RYDE

RYDE

Publisher:

Editors: Triple A Press Books

www.TripleAPressBooks.com

TripleAPress@Mail.com

Final Look Editing

www.finallookediting.com

Finallookediting@gmail.com

Cover Design by: Lane Bellamy

Kahladee

RYDE

Dedication

I dedicate this book to my sons, the two people in this world that I strive to make a difference for. I promise I will do everything within my power to always be a good mother to the both of you. Always know that my love for you is without limitation

RYDE

Acknowledgments

I thank you God for providing me with the strength, courage, passion, and the will power to write. I will continue to learn to love myself, knowing that you will give me the wisdom, clarity, and ambition to keep pushing.

To my mom and dad for making it thru the struggle the realest parent's one could ever have. Thanks for giving me life, without you there would be no me.

Grandma Alberta, One of the greatest loves of my life thank you for always taking care of me and molding me to the women I am, you are the light of my life.

Grandma Bobo, Thank you for always reminding me of how beautiful the heart beats, with you I have always felt safe. When ached for my mother I could look at you and catch a glimpse of her thank you for your part in raising me.

My husband, and father of my sons, I thank you for gifting me with our children, and loving me unconditionally. I love you now and always.

My beautiful intelligent siblings: Tone, thank you for loving me, inspiring me, and pushing me to love when I didn't love myself. Kristin thanks for being who you are and loving me just the way I am. Delphina thank you for always being fair and honest I love you for it.

Kesica you are a one of kind no matter how many ups and downs we go thru we will always have each other.

Reggie thanks for being non-judgmental.

Queie you are the cutest replica of me, I'm still taller.

Tasanee my beautiful niece, I love you meaty mama.

Monte my nephew who is more likes a son you make me proud no matter what.

Lil Marcus my baby boy keeps melting hearts.

Michael even thou it took me some years to realize you were too young to be my dad, I still look up to you.

Nic we have our special bond it's priceless (patty cake).

Marcus you are the only person that can make me feel good about being selfish when it's needed.

Boss ladies my sistas, and friends NaNa, Tasha, Bunny, Barb, Tonya, Lynn, Re Re, Jalonda, Shirlene, Tonda, Kesica, Mellissa I love you all thanks for believing in me, being there for me, keeping it real with me. Nobody runs the town, and own the night like we do cause we BOSSES.

Barbara, Nisha, April, Cozy, Karla, and Tracy Thank you for being true, giving sound advice rather I liked what you had to say or not I love my girls.

To the special people who loved me, consoled me, and motivated me to keep going when I lost the strength, and ability to believe in myself enough. Thanks for making me

Kahladee

feel worthy We are going to shine like the diamonds we are I love you.

Cheri my cover model, you are beautiful.

My sister authors Black Pearll, Fabulous Fe, thanks for sharing your literary world with me. I love you both

My editors Shatona, and Elisha thanks for believing in my story, and
in me.

Lane look at my cover need I say more thank you.

Family and Friends:
Aunt Stephanie, Aunt Juanita, Uncle Leonard, Uncle Paul, Uncle Daryl, Uncle Ronald, Uncle Wayne, Auntee Patricia Anne, Aunt Wendy, Aunt Nita, Mary, Aunt Lottie, Abby Gail, Grandpa Frank, Aunt May, Aunt Loretta, Pee wee, Nan Kimetha, James, Jon-Jon, Jaime, Lil Bit, Jackie, Big Wood, Randal, Laurice, Nince, Emmitt, Ebay, Andre, Pudding, Anthony Ma Brenda, Curtis, Netta, Lisa, Toya, lil Netta, Tan, Mi Mi, Ray Ray, Mills, Aunt Betty, Finest Auntie Linda, Mya, Lavonne, Zebra, Quita, Joyce Black, Rachelle, Bobby, Auntie Ava, Chris, Loraine, Gabby, Trent, Shay, Ken, Zina, Galina, Dasha , Alina, Hanna, Heather, Jessica, Sara, Lana, Natalia, Nadia, Lianne, Sally, Ashley, Essence, Nevin, Katoi, Tiffany, Monet, Leroy, Prentice, Young and Famous, Monica, Lil Monica, Alphonso, Lanaea, Will, Frank, Zink, Missy, Whistle, Anthony, Charelle, Tweet, Victoria, Dustin, Auntie Jill, Twin, Dre, Aunt Margie, Tammy, Xman, Chap, Chico Cartier Bland, Ham, Da Nina Adrienne, Uncle Harold, Aunt Neicy, Akelia, Ryan, Mike Anthony, Tonya, Shatta,

Pye, Tina, Arei, Auntie Dianne, Spud, Vince, Amy, Ernest ,Erica, Daffy, Lena, Tammy, Aunt Helen, Aunt Bird, Helen Helfied, Tonya, Shamelle, Troya, Mrs. Elsie, Juan Juan, Mrs. Marqueta, The Boss Kids, Shaketa, Sharla, Angeline, Jr, Boo, Tine, Kathleen, Baby Mama, Nicole, Gana, Ma Beeks, Missy, Kahalla, Vanilla Ice, Leah, Lando, Luke, Julia, Dawny, Slim, Erica, Anastasia,

Last but not least I want to thank my present and future readers, I'm nothing without you.

"If I forgot anyone please charge it to my head and not my heart."

Kahladee

Chapter 1

Court

"Johnalyn, where the fuck are my keys," Damarie, Johnalyn's boyfriend asked, who happened to be rushing trying to get to court on time. "Shit Nigga, I don't know why I got to help you keep up with your stuff!"

Johnalyn is a mean, fair complicated girl with short sandy brown hair and she has a snappy jealous attitude. Many would consider Johnalyn a "red bone." She has a pretty face and a nice body. She's thick in all the right places, very nicely shaped with deep green eyes. She's only happy when shit goes her way, which is usually all the time when it comes to Damarie. He never wants to fight with or upset her. She held his heart and she knew it. All she had to do was ask and the world was hers. She wanted for nothing and neither did he, they were down for each other.

"Cause you my woman right, J?" Johnalyn hissed back. "Yeah that's right, but I'm not your maid, or your butler!"

Damarie laughs and asks, "Can I take your whip? You know I gotta go to court."

Johnalyn snaps back, "Hell to the naw! I need my car! You know I gotta go see my mama."

"Well drop me off at court then," Damarie responds.

"Damn, I'm not even dressed yet. Now I got to rush up out of here with my hair all over my fucking head looking a mess cause you can't keep up with your shit!"

"J, just hurry the fuck up before a nigga be behind bars, damn!" Johnalyn runs around the apartment collecting her things in her favorite Louis Vuitton duffle bag so she could get ready at her mom's house. Before leaving, she gives the apartment one last scan making sure she didn't forget anything.

Johnalyn and Damarie run down the stairs. They jump into her Acura Integra and speed down Maryland Avenue. Johnalyn continues to press on the accelerator not realizing that she is weaving in and out of traffic.

Damarie shouts, as he clenches the handle on the passenger's door, "Damn J! Let a nigga live, shit!"

Kahladee

"Whatever, motherfucker; you need to just calm the fuck down! Johnalyn glares at him and says "look, just hit me up later and let me know what's popping. Oh yeah, by the way, I'm staying at my place tonight. I'm sure its collecting dust by now. Are you coming over?"

"Naw, you know I can't stay over there! Come on now J quit fronting."

Johnalyn rolling her eyes says, "I'm just saying, you never stay at my crib. I always got to be lugging my shit back and forth to yours."

Johnalyn pulls up to the court house and throws the car in park. Damarie looks at Johnalyn and says, "Listen baby, we'll talk about all this later. I got to appear in front of this judge." Damarie leaned over and kissed J softly on the lips. "Are you sure you don't want to stay at my place tonight?" Damarie gives her a sorry look and just shakes his head.

Get your ass up out my car and I'll talk to you later, nigga."

Damarie stepped out of the car tugging at of his pressed button up shirt making sure he looked presentable before the judge.

Damarie pulled out his 'fit' the night before, being careful not to be too flashy and cocky. He was wearing a pair of taupe colored slacks with a cream colored pull over Polo V-neck sweater to match. Looking decent wasn't a problem for him, in his mind he was a ten. Women found him attractive, too.

Damarie is a naturally handsome young man with a medium muscular build. He wears a goatee. He is pecan brown with dark eyes. His 360° waves just ripple across his dark brown hair. He has long eyelashes, the kind women dream about and his teeth gleam like a Hollywood star with veneers.

"I'm straight," Damarie thought to himself as he entered the packed court room. He nervously glances through the rows and takes the first seat that he sees.

This is the one time he wished his name wasn't Jackson. There were so many cases, before his, Damarie thought it to be ok to rest his eyes. Before long, Damarie had dosed off.

"Damarie Jackson!" The bailiff shouted over the murmuring voices. Damarie jumps up and makes his way up to the stand.

"Do you have representation sir?" The Presiding Judge asks. "Yes sir, Damarie responds, "I will be using the Public Defender appointed to me."

The judge, looking around the courtroom, bellows out, "well where's your attorney at?""

Damarie becoming even more nervous responds, "Well I was told that my lawyer would be here sir." The courtroom doors suddenly fly open, revealing a short bald Caucasian man appearing to be in his late fifties.

Kahladee

Alongside him walks a very attractive African American woman, who looks like she is in her late twenties.

"Excuse us your Honor," the public defender says, "my assistant and I are terribly sorry for being late, it won't happen again, your Honor."

The judge visibly perturbed asks, "Please tell us how your client will plead?"

Damarie thought to himself, "I should have just got a lawyer. Instead, I get an intern and an old ass white dude on my shit and they late and it's my own fucking fault." Damarie feared the worst, even though the maximum time Damarie would have done would be six months to a year.

"My client pleads not guilty Honor."

"Good, the judge replies. Let's proceed then."

The attorney fumbling through papers begins presenting his clients defense.

"Your Honor, the findings show on September 23, 2009 at 8:45 pm, the Washington, D.C. police preformed an illegal search of Mr. Jackson's vehicle. During the search marijuana was found. However, Mr. Jackson bought the vehicle one hour before being pulled over. The police state he was stopped for making a rolling stop at a stop sign. Isn't it possible that the newly purchased used vehicle could have had items left in the car including the marijuana from the previous owners or test drivers of the vehicle?"

"Your Honor, we believe that this charge is outlandish and completely absurd."

"I would like to continue, your Honor, by pointing out that the police searched Mr. Jackson based on his suspicious behavior. He did not want to corporate; therefore, the police deemed it necessary to make a complete search of his car. When they came across the paraphernalia in the glove compartment, Mr. Jackson became uncooperative and the police arrested him based on their finding and failure to corporate with the police."

The Judge, looking over the documents, takes off his glasses and says, "With all due respect Counselor, the search was performed illegally, which gives me no other choice but to throw the case out." The judge rising from his seat hits his gavel and says, "The case against Damarie Jackson is dismissed."

Damarie, smiling with relief, extends his hand and thanks his attorney and his assistant. He then turns and walks towards the bailiff to sign the court dismissal papers.

As the attorney and his legal assistant prepare to leave the courtroom, the attorney turns and looks his legal assistant in the eyes and under his breathe he says, " Don't you ever show up late to court again, especially when you're assigned to be the assistant on my case.

Kahladee

Hey, regardless of the outcome in today's case, your tardiness is inexcusable! The firm I represent will never consider you for a partner."

"Yes sir, never again sir. I'm so sorry. I promise you, it will never happen again."

The attorney walked out of the courtroom without so much of giving his legal assistant acknowledgment for her "work" on the case.

As Damarie walks toward the courtroom door he stops and extends his hand out to shake the legal assistant's hand. "Thank you Ms. Lady! You guys did a great job."

"Yeah well, next time, you might not be so lucky to get a reputable and dedicated firm like this one."

"Dedicated? You call being late dedicated?"

"No, I call that unfortunate just like you will be if you keep this side hustle up without a cover up. But you didn't get that from me. Take care. I gotta run."

Damarie watched her walk away thinking "what the hell does this square know about a side hustle?". He walks out the courtroom doors, smiling in relief that his case was thrown out by the judge. He pulls out his cell phone and calls J.

"What'd they say baby?"

"Oh everything is good, Boo. The judge threw out the case because it was considered an illegal search. Then, listen to this Boo, the police couldn't even prove the fuckin' shit was even mine."

J, says with a sigh of relief, "Thank God we don't have to stress about that anymore.   So what's up for later?"

"Nothing, I'm going home to chill and get ready for these runs that need to be made. Hey, did you change your mind about staying over?"

"No I'm good, J responds, "We will celebrate and chill out later."

"All right then, I love you Boo."

"I love you too baby." J hangs up her cell phone and let's out another sigh of relief.

As Damarie hangs up the phone he remembered he didn't drive. He said to himself, "shit I got to call a ride." He dialed his homeboy Ja'Lee,

What up with it?" Ja'Lee asks.

"Not much man. Can I get a ride?""

"Fo Sho', where you at?"

"I'm at the court house?"

"Oh," Ja'Lee responds, "that's right." "Give me about ten minutes and I'll be there to swoop you up."

Chapter 2

Off Work and Going Out Tonight

Back at the office where Dameta (the legal assistant on Damarie's case) worked, she began to think about her choices. She has taken the bar and passed with flying colors. However, she needed the experience from a top law firm, which she was getting. The problems were that in addition to the hours, the arrogant people like Mr. Smith, who she had court with earlier that day, almost made it seem impossible to be a successful women (let alone a half black woman) in her field, which she knew was the real problem for the firm. They gave her the gritty cases like the drug, prostitution, and troubled inner city juvenile youth cases. Unlike other recent college graduates, who were given major cases against white-collar criminals.

Kahladee

"Ms. Walker, you have a call on line two. Can you take it?"

Dameta snapped out of her thoughts and says, "Yes send the call through please. Thanks."

"This is Dameta Walker, how can I help you"

"Hey girl, what's up, this is Mija."

Dameta smiling says "Hey girl, what's going on?"

"Not much here, Mija responds, just wondering when you would be off and to see if you wanted to grab a bite at Chauncey's Lounge after "Work"?"

"Yeah, that sounds good. I will meet you there."

"Oh no you won't," Mija, hollers back. "It's Friday and we need to go kick it; and, you need to bring your ass home and get out of that tired, boring looking blue skirt suit because it ain't gonna "Work" like that tonight."

"Why you got to talk about my suit? And how do you know if I'm wearing it?"

Mija started laughing before she answered, "Cause you wear it every other Friday! I also saw you leave the crib this morning!"

"Whatever stalker, I'll see you back at home. I will leave in about thirty-minutes. I just need to wrap up a few things here.

"See you then girl."

Dameta hung the phone up and went up to open the office door only to find Mr. Smith there as she swung it open.

"May I help you Mr. Smith?"

"Yes."

"Well what can I do for you?"

"Well you can start by telling my why you were late to trial this morning? Then I need you to tell me why you want to "Work" for Carter, Smith and Getler law firm?"

"Well Sir what happened this morning will never happen again. There is no valid excuse except that I was late due to a transportation issue. As far as my working here, it has always been an honor for me just as I stated in my interview when I was hired. I know I have only tried a handful of cases but I have won every one. That alone, should speak for my abilities and what I can deliver on."

"Well, just don't let happen again. We stand by the names and the meaning of our company and we cannot have anything or anyone getting in the way of that, understood?"

"Yes," she responded firmly, "Understood Sir."

Well that's over and done with for now she thought she looked down and glanced at her watch, damn it's 6:30 already. I'm outta here! I've had enough shit for one day.

Walking up to the door of the condo that she and Mija shared, Dameta could hear the music thumping. Only this Friday, she was not feeling it. She was tired and had an awful day and she just wanted to shower and lay down.

As Dameta walked in, Mija greeted her louder than ever, "Hey girl! Let's get this party started! I already picked you out an outfit. Now hurry and get ready so we can dip."

"I decided I am not going."

"Why not?"

"I'm too tired."

"I knew it was too good to be true," Mija went on. "Damn you need to get out and go on a date. Live a little you haven't been on a date in three years!"

Mija and Dameta could not have been more different. Mija was straight hood and off the fucking chain. She resembled a black Pocahontas. She stood about 5 feet and 7-inches tall. She had a Hershey chocolate complexion with brown eyes. She wore a long weave, which was jet black and parted down the center, not that she didn't have hair she just preferred her weave.

Mija had only finished high school, unlike Dameta, who was very well educated. Mija could have easily gone to college but she opted to run the streets and earned herself a self-proclaimed certificate in street life. She held a job as the Champagne Room Manager at Club Seduce.

One of the personal perks from the club was that Mija had access to a variety of people; hook ups on clothes, jewelry, and too many other things to mention. She used this to her advantage.

Dameta, on the other hand, was only five-feet and three-inches tall. She had light brown eyes and was caramel in complexion. You almost couldn't tell that she was bi-racial. Her mother was Dominican, and her father was Black. Usually you would be able to tell by a person's hair, but not with her. Dameta's hair was thick, cocoa brown in color, and came down to her shoulders. She usually wore it up in a bun with a pair of imitation chopsticks running through it.

"Fine I will get ready, but we are not staying out all night. I have shit to do in the morning."

"Like what, read the paper?" Mija asked sarcastically.

"Just shut up before I change my mind."

Dameta showered and got dressed. Mija had picked out something more revealing than Dameta would have chosen for herself. Mija picked out a gold sequence tank top that hung low, a pair of tight fitting boot cut Seven jeans and a pair creamed colored wedge sandals.

You had to give it to Mija. She could dress her ass off and tonight was no different; she was wearing a short black dress with strappy heels.

Mija gave Dameta some confidence when she said "Damn you look good in common clothes now let's roll out this mutha."

They were on their way to the restaurant Chauncey's. Since Chauncey's was only four blocks away from their loft, they just walked. Everybody went there because the food was bomb and they had live music.

The line at Chauncey's was long and it was flooded with a mix of people but mainly people with money of some sort. Those that didn't have money came with people who did.

"We should have made reservations Mija."

"Girl, you really need to learn how to just chill out. Give it a minute. We will get in. Wait right here a second." Mija said as she made her way past the crowd and up toward the front of the line. Mija was trying to see who the host was. She saw that it was Caleb. "Oh we good," she thought to herself. So she turned around and headed back toward Dameta.

"Let me use your cell Dameta". She called inside the restaurant. Caleb answered.

"Hey Caleb, this is Mija. Me and my girl are stuck in this long ass line. Can you help us out baby?"

"Well what's in for me?"

"I got you Boo. How 'bout two free dances in the champagne room?"

"Cool. Go ahead and walk to the side door and I will send someone in a second."

Once they were in and seated it was cool and popping. Dameta didn't see one familiar face; but, Mija on the other hand knew everyone.

Before they could even order a drink someone had sent two shots of Patrón over to their table. Mija asked the waitress who sent these and the waitress pointed across the room to a guy wearing black slacks and a white button up.

"Do you know him Dameta?"

"I sure as hell, don't. I think he is one of your peeps Mija,"

"Aw no," Mija giggled, "Not dressed like that!" They both started laughing.

"He is kind of cute though huh?" Mija said.

Dameta agreed, and then scolded Mija and said "Don't be rude. Pick up the shot glass and thank the man for the drinks.

That was his cue. He walked over and introduced himself. "Good evening a lady, my name is Mega and how are you doing tonight? I hope the shots were ok?"

Kahladee

Mija continued doing the talking for her and Dameta "Well they were cool, considering you don't even know if we drink Patrón."

"Well I made a lucky guess." Just as Mega turned to make eye contact with Mija, shots rang out.

"What the fuck!" Mija screamed. "Let's go Dameta, now! They are shooting this mutha fucka up."

Mija grabbed Dameta by the hand and made her way towards the front door. People were running in every direction bumping and stomping into each other; it was like a riot broke out. By the time she reached the door all you could see was smoke and at least three people were lying on the ground. Dameta, panting and out of breath, shouted at Mija. "See this is why I don't go out no damn where, don't ask me again."

"Girl shut up! Let's just go home!"

They ran two blocks up the street looking back at the scene,

"Well we can walk now all we got is two blocks to go,"

Mija said. They slowed down and started walking

Mija, heavily out of breath asked Dameta "what the fuck just happened?"

Dameta out of breath as well replied, "Shit, who you asking?"

As they approached the end of the block Dameta saw what she thought was homeless man doubled over but the closer she got she noticed it was a young Black man holding his side.

"Girl just walk by cause we don't know this fool," Mija said, walking a little faster.

"No, Mija. Let's help him."

Dameta hunched over and said to the man, "Sir, are you ok? Sir, are you ok?

"Yeah, I'm cool;" the man said groaning. "I got shot at the club."

Dameta grabbed her phone, "Let me call an ambulance." the man groaned out "No police or ambulance. Just get me somewhere so we can look at this." The man continued to groan.

Mija looked at Dameta rolled her eyes and said, "See, you be fucking up. We don't know him."

"Just help him girl. We live close; we only got another block and half."

Mija grabbed him under one arm and Dameta under the other. They held him up until they made it to their loft. Once inside, they helped him lie down on the couch, and they noticed that there was a small amount of blood on the side of his shirt. Mija helped him take his shirt off.

Kahladee

"Well looks to me that you were grazed pretty good but not shot thank God," Mija said as she was still inspecting his wounds.

While Mija was getting the man settled, Dameta went to get towels, peroxide, alcohol, hot water, and bandages.

They both helped clean him up and then Mija left to find him a clean T-shirt to put on. Dameta could not help but to look at him. He was fine as hell, "damn" she thought. She blanked out for a minute and then said "well, would you like something to drink?"

"Yeah, please."

She went to the fridge and grabbed a bottle of water and a Gatorade to offer him. He opted for the water and said "Thank you."

Dameta couldn't keep her eyes off him and finally said

"You look real familiar."

"Yeah I was thinking the same about you what your name is?"

"Dameta," she stated. "What's yours?"

"Damarie."

"Damarie? Oh my god! I had your case this morning."

"Shit you that square lawyer."

"I'm not so square now, am I?"

"No. You're not at all. Forgive me, but you look real different in your business suit." She laughed sarcastically.

"Well I see you two are getting acquainted." Mija said as she passed him the T-shirt. It wasn't long before Mija also noticed how fine he was. Before, they could continue their fantasies about him. He abruptly said "Well ladies, I thank you for everything. I think I'm good now. Let me at least pay you or something."

"No it's good. Can we call you a cab or something?" Dameta asked him.

"No. But, do you mind if I could use your phone so I can get a ride?" Dameta handed him her cell phone.

Damarie quickly called J.

"Hey baby, it's me."

"Where the fuck is you at? she spat" I have been blowing you up for the last hour. You said you were going home. I went by there and you weren't even there; and, whose phone are you calling from?"

"Babe, listen. I went to Chauncey's and there was an altercation. I got a graze wound. These ladies were nice enough to help me. Now will you pick me up? I will explain everything later.

"Where are you at?"

28

"Hold on I will get the address. Hey Miss lady, what's your address?"

Dameta replied, 4505 6th Street.

J says "Them lofts?

"Yeah, J"

"Who you know there?" J asked.

Frustrated, and tired of questions Damarie raises his voice and responds "Just come on, damn!"

J locked the phone number under the name "Loft Hoe." She ran down the stairs and jumped into her car and began speeding off down the street. She left in such a hurry she didn't realize that she was still in her pajamas and wearing her headscarf.

After Damarie hung up the phone, he said "Thank you both again, let me leave you my number."

"Fucking liar!" J thought and she continued to speed down the street. She was pissed.

While Damarie waited on J he wrote his digits down and passed them right to Dameta. He told Dameta and Mija, "If you ever need a favor or if you want to go to lunch some time, hit me up." There was a honk of the horn and he limped off toward the door waving bye one final time.

"Hey Mija" Dameta said whispering after she heard the door shut. It has been a hell of a night! This is why I don't go out! Who got time for this kind of drama?"

"Yeah girl" it has certainly been crazy Mija replied.

But "Fuck drama! Ole boy fine as hell, I would call him if I was you."

"Ahh, did you not witness him call his girl on the phone?"

"Yeah, but I also heard her mouthing off and being all agitated. That's not what keeps a man, If I were her I would be like, I'm on my way to make it all better boo, as fine as he is."

"Yeah I bet you would, crazy ass girl." Dameta replied.

Chapter 3

Your Place or Mine

"So what happened, Damarie; and you better begin by telling me the truth"

"Babe, I do not even know. Like I said to you over the phone, I was at Chauncey's networking; and you know, making some moves."

"What happened Damarie? Who were you with?"

"I was with Ja'Lee; but, then he got a call and had to make a run. I didn't want to go with him cause like I said I was making my own moves up in Chauncey's. I had just chopped it up to one of my homie's, you know, Mega; about possibly doing some moves. We did what we needed to do, he went his way and I went mine. Shit, the next thing I know somebody starting shooting up the place. I don't know who the bullets was intended for, but I rolled out walking fast as hell and got grazed any mutha fucking way."

"Shit Damarie they was probably for Mega's ass. You know he's hot as hell out here."

"Like I said J, I don't know. I was just trying to get the fuck up out of there. I lost my phone and everything. J, I was in so much pain that I just fell over and that's when those girls came walking up and helped a nigga out. So why are you tripping?" Now, I am worried about my phone so let's get to my crib and get it shut off. I don't want my connects and shit just out there all afloat."

"I got them all in my phone Damarie so why you worried because for one they all under fake names?"

Let's just go to my crib to turn it off, dang."

"No!" J shot back, "We are going to my place because I left my lights and shit on. Babe do you know how much shit I got in my crib right now? Obviously you don't. Shit, we fuck around get robbed then what?"

"Fine we will go to your crib."

Once back at Damarie's, J called the phone company to report the phone stolen just like he told her too.

"Damarie, lets lay down. We got to get up damn early tomorrow."

J says "What you mean?

Damarie reminds her, "You know we got to make that run, and now we got to grab me a new cell.

J complaining says, "Damn can't we do it Sunday. It's already four in da morning?"

Damarie doesn't play when it comes to his paper and says "No, we can't so let's lay down like I said."

They both headed down the hall to Damarie's room. J jumped in Damarie's king size bed and peeled out of her clothes. While undressing, she winks at him and made a come here motion with her index finger.

Damarie climbed in and began to kiss her starting at her feet making his way up until he reached her lips were he begin to kiss her softly teasing her with his tongue.

"What you got for Daddy, Ma?"

"Anything you want Boo."

"I want you Ma."

Damarie flipped over on his back landing J on top on him.

"Take daddy for a ride, Ma

J leaned over Damarie squatting down on his dick. He was rock hard, wide and long even though she had been with him for years she could never get used to the way he felt to her, it was as if every time was her first with him. She damn there jumped off as she sat on.

"Baby you hurt so good,"

"I do Ma?"

"Yes daddy."

"That's good Ma.   Keep going." She did until they both came, and fell asleep.

Damarie woke up about 9:00 O'clock AM the next morning letting J sleep in a little longer. He headed to the kitchen, poured himself a glass of juice and took out some English muffins, bacon, eggs, and cheese. Damarie whipped up a quick breakfast, ate and then headed back to the room to serve J breakfast in bed.   She was still asleep.

"J, wake up baby, we gotta get a move on.

When she opened her eyes; Damarie teasingly said, "Damn Boo, I put it on you like that?"

"Yeah, something like that." J replied not wanting to give him his props.   Damarie ignores her sarcasm and shoving the plate in her face "Here eat. I'm going to hop in da shower and when you're finished come and jump in the shower with me so we can bounce Babe."

By the time they showered and got dressed it was 11:00 o'clock AM. Damarie usually liked to hit the road to do his run by 7am on the third Saturday of the month to pick up his product. Although there was plenty of clientele around DC, major paper was made in New Jersey. He

Kahladee

made the 3-hour drive every month even though it was a big risk. The money was just too good to let go.

"Thank God, I found my keys because if we took your car that's an automatic red flag by them dicks just because of those dumb personalized plates I told your ass not to get J"

 Damarie pushed his all black 2008 Tahoe on black 24-inch rims on the highway like it was a limousine. Damarie was usually careful not to speed but he did 80-mph trying to make up for lost time , bumping the newest Tone Mitch CD. He is a Midwest underground artist, on the way to become the latest big rap sensation. It was in his mother's name and she resided in Jersey, which made it a little easier to dodge the cops.

 J was laid back in the passenger seat talking on her cell non-stop to her girl Raneka about the latest gossip. Raneka and J had known each other for only about a year but had hit it off when they met each other at Nara's hair salon, in fact Raneka was going through a bad a break up at the time. So J hooked her up with Ja'Lee, they made a cute couple. Ja'Lee was light skinned and handsome despite the fact that he was a little on the pudgy side. Raneka was pretty cute. She was short and dark in complexion. She carried herself well, usually wore her hair in an asymmetrical bob. She and J stayed laced in all the newest gear. Staying laced was easy for the two comrades as they both held good paying jobs. To top it off their men had loot. At times it seemed like they were in competition with each other. J always seemed to remind Raneka in some way or another that if it wasn't for her, she would have never met Ja'Lee'. The truth was they had less in common than they initially thought and only hung out now because Ja'Lee and Damarie were boys.

They had known each other since the 7th grade and their bond was tighter than rubber bands. They never made any major business deals without each other; the only thing they could potentially end up clashing about was J. Ja'Lee never thought J was good for Damarie. In fact he always knew J had another side to her but never wanted to scar his friendship with Damarie. And he knew Damarie had loved J since 9th grade. So he supported his Damarie's decision to be with J.

Once Damarie hit the Jersey line it was about 4:00 o'clock PM. Damarie called "Work" his connect on his new phone..."Hello who dis?" Work answered

"Dis me" Damarie says.

"Oh OK, I thought you wasn't coming. You have never been dis late."

Damarie sighs and says "I know it's a long story, I'm going to drop my Boo off at my mom's and come through alright?"   Damarie never brought J with him to "Work's" house even though she knew the business and helped

---

him move weight; if anything ever went down, he did not want her to reap the repercussions.

"Damarie, I want you to hurry back because your mother will have fifty million questions. I am not feeling it today so do not try to sit and chill."

"Yeah, I hear you, I'm going there and coming right back." Damarie said as he turned down the music as he pulled in his mom's driveway. He rushed J out the car telling her to hurry up so he could drive away before his mom saw him .J walked to the door and rang the bell. Damarie's mom, Belle, opened the door surprised to see J. "Oh my, hi, I'm glad you made it" Ms. Belle began peeping her head around J trying to spot Damarie. "Where's Damarie?"

"Oh, he will be here in just a few. He went to meet up with a friend for a drink" J told her

"Oh well, this will be a good time for us to chat and catch up. I tried calling you guys but I did not get an answer. I thought you weren't coming considering you guys are never here this late."

"Oh I must have had my phone on silent; and, Damarie drove with the music up so loud he probably didn't hear his." J knew she saw and heard Belle's calls the whole time but just rejected them. His mom asked too many questions and J could only tolerate so much.

"Well you must be starving. The food is done so let's sit down and eat. I made roast, cornbread, cabbage and peach cobbler; all of Damarie's favorites."

J sat down to eat and before she could take a bite, the questions started.

"So J, are you two getting closer to marriage? I hope so because I am ready to be a grandma. I just don't know what you guys are waiting on. You have been together a long time." Before J could answer, Ms. Belle popped another question.

"Your mother and I can't wait to plan the wedding with you of course."

"Well Mrs. Belle, Damarie and I are just fine we don't talk about marriage often. We like to travel, we are busy all the time; and as far as kids are concerned, well the subject hasn't even crossed either of our minds.

J knew she was only lying to herself. She wanted to be Damarie's wife and mother of his kids ever since she could remember. He was the one that wasn't ready, always in the streets paper chasing, hustling and looking for more ways to come up. But in J's mind they had come up, they had nice cars, apartments, money in the bank, 2 rental houses that no one knew anything about but them. They only rented them out to keep a low profile. J was tired of taking risk-running dope, slinging dope, but she wasn't tired of the fast money. She longed for normalcy. She wanted to have her family and friends over without worrying about something awful happening. And there

Kahladee

was the fear Damarie instilled in her about being robbed, snitched on, and hurt because people were jealous about the fact that he was rising in the streets making a name for himself .He always reminded J never to tell people who her man was as he was afraid someone would hurt her. Even though she knew the game he only let her deal with the females and he dealt with the males that kept down confusion, hearsay and the risk of them loosing each other to bullshit.

Chapter 4

Meeting with "Work"

Damarie meets with "Work." "What up, "Work"?

"Work" responds "Nothing partner, chillin'.

How is business?" Damarie says.

"Oh, you know how it is. It's all good until somebody doesn't want to pay." "Work replies."

"Well you know that's never the case with me." Damarie proudly exclaims.

"Yeah, Damarie, if everybody was real in the game like you, we would not have problems. So what are we doing?" "Work asked Damarie. "Can I get you a drink?"

Damarie responds, "no man I'm good, I'm behind schedule, let me get my usual, and I'll be up out your way."

"Cool," "Work" says and hit the intercom for his butler to bring the keys to the vault. "Work" lived in a small mansion out in the burbs of Jersey. It was "tricked out," he had a few servants, and staff members that worked for him and his wife who was half white and Indonesian. His wife came from money and didn't have a clue what her husband did on the side to supplement their income. She thought he just worked for her father. Nevertheless, for the most part they led a low key life and he didn't need a cover up because he had a couple of businesses with his father-in-law and to be real he was white and no one would have ever suspected that he was doing anything illegal.

The Butler walked in with the keys to the vault. Damarie usually waited until "Work" got back from the vault with the "product", but this time, "Work" offered Damarie to, "come back with him and have a drink or a glass of wine. We've been doing business too long for you not to relax, I trust you." Damarie followed "Work" around the corner of a book shelf and to his surprise there was a fake door that opened to a gliding walk way.

"Work" looked at Damarie and said "hop on, but watch your step." The moving walkway came to a stop in the round shaped foyer. There were three labeled doors, one was labeled "Spa," the others were "Dad's Space," and

"Wine Cellar." Damarie thought "Damn, I knew he was doing well, but not this well."

"Work" opened the door to the room labeled "Frozen Wine Cellar." "Work" had every wine, and vodka you could name in there. The room's temperature was subzero, but it was "decked out," with a pub style table, Ice bar, and love seat, it even had a minks on the coat racks just for people to wear while drinking in the cellar.

"Damn, man, this is crazy!" Damarie stated, not meaning to say his feelings aloud, but since he had, he continued. "What were you thinking when you built this?"

"Work" replied, "strictly entertainment for the wife and her friends. Anything to keep her busy and out my business, you know what I mean?"

"Yeah I feel you." Damarie replied.

"Work" chuckled at Damarie's amazement and said "sit down, grab a fur let's have a drink." Damarie sat at the bar

"Work" poured him a glass of some old aged French cognac and offered him a Cuban cigar.

As Damarie lights the cigar, "Work" looks up and says, "I've been thinking, Damarie, I want to do more business with you. I like how you handle yours; I never hear your name in the streets, you have small team and that's how I like to operate."

"So what are you thinking "Work"?" Damarie asked.

Kahladee

"I'm thinking of going international. I'm not trying to work for her pops the rest of my life. To keep it real, I don't plan on catering to her or her rich ass dad too much longer that's why I keep her out my business." "Work" replied.

So you want to go international? Damarie said aloud because he wasn't sure what to say.

"Work" tried to reassure him. "Well, it's not going to be easy, but we could do it. All I need is for you to say, is yes."

"Man, "Work," I feel you but I gotta think about this one. Give me some time to think about this."

"Work" replied "that's fine, take your time, but try not to keep me waiting too long."

"Work" then said "I'll be right back" and walked to the vault room and grabbed the "product." Damarie put out his cigar and took one last sip of his wine. "Thanks "Work," I will be in touch."

"Work" led Damarie through the Spa room, which led out to the outdoor patio and from there "Work" led him to his vehicle.

Damarie hopped in his truck, turned down the music and thought to himself, "damn, international, I didn't see that coming. But I gotta think about it; I'm doing well, but I can do better. After a few runs, I can be out the game and kick back, and really start living." Then J crossed his mind, "She is never going to go for this. She already complains about riding to Jersey, I'm not even going to bring this to her tonight. I'm going to sit on it a few days."

Once back at his moms it was already, 8 o'clock at night. Mama Belle came right to him and said "Baby, you look tired let me make you a plate so you can eat, and relax." J rolled her eyes in the back of her head, "Mama Belle, I can do it." "No, honey, you're tired too, relax, I got it." Damarie sat down to eat and was talking to his mom while J, texted on her BlackBerry. By the time Damarie and his mom finished talking it was 9'oclock. Damarie feeling bad for J said, "Well mom, we better hit the road it's late."

Mama Belle replied, "No honey, why don't you guys stay here tonight and leave in the morning after breakfast?"

Damarie looked at J, he could tell she did not want to but the fact was, he was tired. "You know what mom, you're right, I'm beat. We'll just stay here tonight."

J's face almost turned to stone. "Uhh!" She thought to herself. Then said to Damarie, "Baby, we don't even have clean clothing"

"Well, we can put the same duds back on in the morning. It's not going to kill us. I know I got plenty of T-shirts you can sleep in."

Belle spoke and said, "I will get your rooms ready Damarie you can sleep in your room. Dameta you can sleep in the spare just let me change the sheets. Don't

Kahladee

you two give me those confused looks you know I don't play that shacking up" "Mom you're the one always talking about how you want grandkids and all."

Damarie was making a joke cause he knew J was pissed, Belle started down the hall to get the rooms ready. "J chill don't worry soon as she falls asleep I'm going to sneak to your room, we are grown we should not have to sneak. However, this is her house, besides its fun. Now I have to call Ja'Lee so he can stay at the crib or at least check stuff out."

Damarie picked up his cell and dialed Ja'Lee he answered on the first ring, "What's good?"

"Shit, still chilling at my mom's we going to stay tonight I'm tired from all that shit that popped off at Chauncey's, the drive, and the whole nine. "So what are you getting into tonight?" Damarie asked

"Nothing, just chilling with my baby, we are kicked back tonight." Ja'Lee responded.

"Man I don't want to interrupt, but will the two of you chill at my crib tonight?"

"Yeah, it should be cool, let me tell Raneka before she gets too comfy. Otherwise, how was the concrete today?" Ja'Lee asked.

Damarie reassured him and said "It was good nobody got out of hand, no fights, everything was chill."

"Good to hear" Ja'Lee replied.

Not wanting to hold him, Damarie said, "Well, I'm going to let you go thanks man."

Morning rolled around quick. Damarie woke up to the smell of breakfast; he looked at the clock next to his bed. "10:00 AM, already damn," he sprung up grabbed a shirt and headed out to the hall. He heard his mom talking on the phone, so he headed straight to the guest room. He opened the door and J was wide awake. She looked at Damarie, "well nice of you to join me," J, said.

"I can't even lie, boo, I was knocked out by the time I hit the sheets." He leaned over and kissed her on the forehead. "I will make it up to you." Damarie promised.

"Well, get up Ma, let's go eat. My mom is in the kitchen putting it down as usual." Damarie said to J.

J no longer could resist her stomach pangs and rose out of bed "sounds like a plan to me." After breakfast, Damarie and J showered, threw on yesterday's clothes, said their good byes, and hit the freeway.

Kahladee

Chapter 5

Back to the Gravel

Damarie hit a few blocks before going all the way home just to see who and what was on the streets. It was live for a Sunday afternoon. As he pulled into the underground parking lot to his apartment building he thought about how much work he had to do. J was about to be tripping. But "oh well," he thought, this is what she signed up for.

J grabbed the duffle bag and thought to herself, "He just doesn't know that I am not going with him on any more of his runs out of town. I'm going to let him know that I'm ready to stop this risk taking. I'm going to help him get these last birds sold and that's it."

Once in the house they both sat on the couch with a sigh of relief. "Damarie we need to talk."

"'Bout what Ma?" Damarie responded.

"About all of this! J spat back at him "What more do you want out of this life? I'm tired of this life style Damarie! "Tired of what exactly J? he asked obviously agitated at her. "Eating good, dressing nice, new whips, houses, trips, what part are you tired of Ma?" Damarie said with a bit of an attitude.

"The risk, Damarie; and always being paranoid; and not going the places I want to go; and most of all, I seriously want to be a wife and a mother."

""All that's to come J; you just need to have patience with me. It's not like you want a little house on the hill and; a small wedding. You an extravagant lifestyle and wedding." Damarie reminded her.

"Yes, I want nice things, but not at the cost of my freedom and my life with you. Have you considered slowing down Damarie?"

"No, actually, I have plans on picking up the pace, since you asked. There's money to be made and I'm about to go harder than I ever have before." Damarie responded.

"Well you can count me out. I'm done with the shit after we flip these last birds." J said.

Kahladee

"What you mean, you done J? We got mortgages, rents and all type of shit to pay for.""

J rolling her eyes at Damarie responds "I mean I want out of this hustle! I have a job or did you forget?"

"No, I didn't forget J. But that job ain't going to allow you the lifestyle you want to live."

"So what are you saying Damarie? I'm not entitled to what's already here? I helped you build this shit! You didn't do this alone nigga. Or, have you forgotten?"

"I didn't forget but J, you knew what you signed up for when we drove down this road."

We supposed to be together on this Ma. Look Ma, we going to talk later because I'm not feeling you and you aren't feeling me on this."

"As far as I'm concerned this conversation is done Damarie. I'm out of the game. I'm your woman and you need to make me your wife real soon."

"Yeah, I hear you J. You out and that's enough said. Later, I got moves to make."

Damarie grabbed some of the work he brought back, and stormed out the front door, slamming it the door so hard, the windows shook. He was pissed at J for the first time in long time. She was starting to annoy him with the attitude and the whining.

"Damarie was talking out loud to himself as he walked out the apartment complex, "she got me fucked up right now with all this baby, and marriage talk. She knows we can't raise a baby in this life. What's she thinking about? I swear she watch too much damn TV."

Damarie jumped in the truck called Ja'Lee up and told him to meet him for a drink at Chauncey's. Ja'Lee rolled up in his 2008 Audi A7. Damarie got out the truck, shook up with Ja'Lee, and proceeded to go in the restaurant. As soon as they were seated, Damarie ordered three shots of goose.

"Damn Damarie, it's like that? Ja'Lee asked.

"Hell yeah, man. J tripping, talking this shit 'bout she want out of this game."

"What man?" Ja'Lee was shocked.

"Yeah, that's exactly what I said, Ja'Lee." Damarie replied.

"Well Damarie, what you want from me, my ear, or advice?

"Both bro." I say let her out cause you know when the hunger is gone then carelessness takes place. Why she want out all of a sudden?" Ja'Lee inquired.

Kahladee

"I don't know what bitch been in her ear but she talking marriage, baby, and all that. Some shit, she know we're not ready for." Damarie added.

"I feel you on that because I'm not ready either" Ja'Lee' agreed.

They looked at each other at the same time and said "I'm just ready to get this paper."

"See great minds think alike," Damarie chuckled. This brings me to the new business at hand. "Work" says he got plans to take things international, I told I him I would get back to him but, I'm ready. What about you Ja'Lee?"

"Well you know I'm down, Damarie. Did you even have to ask? But this also means we need to increase our team because it's still money to be made on the concrete and we can't be local and international at the same time. Yeah I know, we definitely going to need another female, one that will grit just as hard as J but minus that slick ass mouth and attitude." Ja'Lee suggested.

"Right playa, but we need some muscle too, have anybody in mind?" Damarie asked.

"Yeah actually I do.'" Ja'Lee said.

"Who?" Damarie inquired.

"Mega..." Ja'Lee replied.

"Mega, that just got out of jail?" Damarie asked.

"Yeah I ran into him the other night at the store. I talked to him for a hot minute and we were supposed to meet up, but I got busy.

"That's funny you saw him because I talked to him at Chauncey's the other night right before the shooting"

"My only concern Ja'Lee about bringing him in is that nigga is a lil' too trigger-happy and he kind of hot on the streets."

"Yeah I know, but his heat really came from some disloyal niggas and that can happen to anyone that doesn't have a real team of loyalty." Ja'Lee.

Damarie reluctantly said "Alright put him in, but local first."

"As far as a female who are you thinking 'bout Damarie?"

"Ja'Lee, I haven't thought about it cause J just resigned a hour ago, but I'm going to work on that cause you know that even though she not in, J's still going to try to run shit."

Damarie's phone rang. He looked down at it, saw it was J and hit the ignore button. "There she go blowing me up now, after I told her I was about to make some moves."

"Man, I feel you sometimes Raneka get on that same shit but want to stay shopping at the mall, and want a nigga under her ass at the same time."

Kahladee

"Man who you telling J think she owns the mall, "Well, I suppose we better hit the blocks and do what we do best; get this paper you take east and I will hit the west side shake things up a bit." Damarie stated.

"Alright bet, later" Ja'Lee responded and threw a fifty on the table. "This one is on me bro."

By the time Damarie made it home it was 2 in the morning. To his surprise J was still up watching some wedding reality show on TV. He thought to himself, "Yeah this is where she getting all this dumb ass shit from.

"Ma, you got to work in the morning."

"Yeah I do, but I can't sleep, too much on my mind Damarie."

"Well ease your mind, cause we good. I understand where you coming from, you out, like you wanted, you got my blessing, but all this baby and marriage talk going to have to wait a while because I got some things in the making."

"But Damarie, what's the point of me getting out, if I can't have what I want with you?"

"You can have what you want with me, just not within the next year. Ma, I'm just not ready for kids. You can take the rest of this year and start doing things you want to with yourself whether it be going back to school, taking trips, starting a business or whatever. Cause you going to have to get all that out your system because once you have my seed, all that mall hopping is not going to be going down. You going to stay home and raise mine."

Damarie peeled out of his clothes, jumped in bed, and fell fast asleep.

Chapter 6

Build a Bigger Team

The next morning Damarie woke up and J was already gone. He rolled over and saw she had left a note for him. He picked it up and read it.

"Damarie thank you for understanding, I know I'm going to make a good wife and even better mother. Love always your future wifey."

Even though Damarie didn't understand where this was all coming from, he just accepted and respected it for what it was.

He got out of bed and picked up the house a little bit, looked at his phone and there were eight missed calls.

Three of the calls were from Mega and the other five were from J. He hit J back first, "What's up Mama?"

"Nothing baby, I was just seeing if you wanted to go to lunch today?"

"No actually, I can't. I gotta meet up with one of the fellas from the block."

"Who?" J asked.

"Chill, with the questions Ma, you out now, that means, just work your job, find a hobby and keep up your beauty."

"Damn baby, why so harsh? J said.

"I don't mean to be J, but I want you to focus on the things I asked you, not what I'm doing. I love you and we'll go out for dinner later alright?"

Still a little taken aback, J replied "Yeah, ok later."

When he hung up the phone, he realized that maybe came off a little' harsh. Damarie showered got dressed, and called Mega back, "what's up Mega?"

"Not much man, sorry for blowing you up. I was just making sure we were still on for lunch today."

"Yeah we still on. I was knocked out cold. I had a long weekend."

"OK, when and where?" Mega asked.

"Let's meet up at about one downtown at Phatties Bistro."

Kahladee

"All right, bet." Mega agreed.

Damarie hung up the phone and headed downtown early so he could send J some flowers from the flower shop across the street from the bistro.

He walked in and ordered a mix of calla lilies, and roses. When the clerk asked what he wanted the card to read he told her to write, "I love you, I miss you and you're the only women for me." He paid extra to have them delivered to her job the same day.

As he walked out the flower shop, he looked at his watch and he still had plenty of time before Mega was to arrive but he decided to head over to Phatties anyway.

He started to walk across the street, saw a familiar female face; they locked eyes as they drew closer. Damn, that's ole girl from the other night. She almost brushed past him, but he grabbed her hand and said "so we meet on the street again huh?"

She looked at him snatching her hand back "excuse me, do I know you?"

He answered her question sarcastically "oh, you got amnesia now? What, you help so many random people you don't remember a face?"

"Oh yeah, now I remember. I didn't notice you because you're not all bent over, crying, or in court" she chuckled. "Your name again?"

"Damarie and yours?"

"It's Dameta. Well I was just heading over to Phatties. Dameta, let me buy you lunch as repayment for helping me. I really did appreciate your hospitality."

She stood there contemplating if she wanted to be seen in public with a past client. "Well, I have to be back to work in forty five minutes"

"Come on baby girl, its lunch not a five course meal." "Alright, let's do it." She agreed.

Damarie called up Mega. Man, something came up; can you meet me around two instead?

"Yeah, it's cool, we good."

They were seated and ordered right away. Dameta had a salad and Damarie ordered a Reuben.

"So tell me about yourself, Dameta since you know a lil' about me. How long you been practicing law?"

"Six years and I still haven't made associate or partner."

"Why is that?"

"Seriously, I don't know. I have never lost a case; to be honest I believe it's a race, gender, and class thing. How many young black, Dominican, female lawyers do you know?"

"Well, just one."

Kahladee

"My point exactly, and I worked my ass off to get where I'm at. My grandmother raised me back in Atlanta, and trust me it was not easy me being biracial in the South."

"Not to pry but where are your parents Dameta?"

"I was an army brat until they were killed in a car accident when I was nine; my mother was black and my dad was Dominican. Well enough about me what about you?"

"Well I'm from New Jersey originally, I moved here when I graduated high school with my girlfriend. We are high school sweethearts, My mom still lives there , and as far as my dad I couldn't tell you never met him. He ran off when my mom was pregnant."

You could tell by the silence, that they had both touched sore spots.

"So Dameta, do you have your own clientele?"

"No my contracts forbid me to do so unless someone specifically request me."

"Well you got me off with no problem can you be my personal lawyer?"

"Yeah about that, how about you plan on making sure no new cases occur?"

"Well that sounds all good, but the reality is in my line of work, it's destined to happen again." He said.

"Look as a lawyer; I can't promote what you do because it is breaking the law. However, if you are my client, it would be my job to believe and represent you. I am going to go on a whim and give you some advice and information. When I researched your case, I did a little digging and I discovered they're not looking at you, but they will start now. My advice to you is to start a business of some sort.

You need a money front, one that generates revenue. In the meantime, if you have any problems, or questions here is my card, call me. I understand that you got to make a living, and I can tell that your clean about it which is a good thing, but remember it's always the smallest mistakes that we make that we suffer the deepest lost from.

Not putting assets in your name seems to be the right path to take. If the name the asset is listed under is someone who can afford it. Can your girl really afford two homes, a new car, and be able to lease two apartments? And your mother, can she really afford her home and your vehicles? These are the kind of things that will come back to haunt you in the long run. And then everyone goes down."

Damarie looked at her like he was at a loss for words, but he didn't want to seem like he was completely aloof, so he spoke up, "Damn, you just turned my whole point of thinking around, I appreciate your advice and I will be thinking of ways to use it."

"Well good sir, but I must be going back to work now thank you for lunch."

Kahladee

"Oh, it was my pleasure Dameta, you can call me anytime you need to talk or if you just want to hang out and vent about work."

"Be careful what you ask for. I just might take you up on that," she smiled as she walked away from the table.

As she walked off, she could not help to think who ever that woman that has the pleasure of pleasing him is one lucky lady.

Mega was walking in as Dameta was on her way out. He looked back and thought "she's cute, I think I seen her somewhere before," he made nothing of it and strolled back to where Damarie was sitting and said "Hey what's cracking with you player?"

"Nothing man, just ready to get this money."

"I feel you because I know I am." Mega said.

Mega was tall and stalky, had a handsome face, and a few noticeable tattoos, but he could use some help in the wardrobe department. His lack of fashion sense was really due to the time he had been in prison. He hadn't caught up with what was "in" and "out," he had only been out of prison six months from serving five years in the state penitentiary.

"I have been wanting to work with you a long time Damarie, you're loyal and you run your team with respect. I never hear of any beefs with your squad."

"That's all true Mega because everybody eats on my team and there's never a shortage, and if there is, we get right down to it."

I want to bring you in Mega but there are some things I'm skeptical about, such as, your beefs, known and unknown, your gang affiliation, and you're hotheaded plus trigger-happy."

"With all due respect Damarie I had to cut my losses and I no longer have beefs with anyone that I know of people just weren't loyal to me that's why I took all the cases. I didn't go snitching and name dropping. As far as the gang affiliation, I'm not no underboss, I'm a boss. I put in my work, that's my family and they going to be for me and rest assure there won't be any problems that arise, that I can't dismember."

"Enough said Mega, you're in, anyone you consider putting on, has to come through me and Ja'Lee . I want you to work the north side of town. I only cover a few blocks there, but I want more. Keep in mind, I expect you to recruit clientele, and be in the loop of everything north. I will plug you up with Ja'Lee later this evening so you can get your product, meet the existing clientele, and show you which blocks were looking to get into."

Damarie ordered Mega a couple of drinks, and lunch to welcome him to the team, they made small talk, and left. Mega feeling like he was a part of something real, Damarie wondering if he had made a mistake.

Kahladee

Damarie got in the truck, hearing his phone ring he picked it up out of the console it was J, he answered "yeah boo, what's up?"

"I been calling and texting you forever baby where you been?"

"I told you I had to meet up with someone."

"Oh yeah, that's right. Well anyway, thank you so much for my flowers. They are beautiful. All the girls were so jealous. I love you baby, what time you going to be home?"

He looked at his watch and saw it was already four o' clock. "I got a couple more things to do so it will be about six or six thirty."

"OK, are we still on for dinner?"

"Yeah, we can do that, make reservation somewhere around eight. That way, I got time to get dressed."

"Ok Damarie, Love you, bye."

"Love you too, J, see you around six"

Once he hung up from J, Ja'Lee was calling. He answered, "I was just about to call you bro."

"Well, no need because I called you, what up with it?" "Not much, I met with our new teammate today and I need you to take him to the north side and get him set up tonight."

"Sounds good, just hit me with his number and I am on it. What else you got going on bro?"

" Nothing right now, Ja' Lee"

"Well let's go grab a haircut Damarie; you know we got to stay fresh to death."

"You fucking right, till the last breath. I will see you there.

.

Chapter 7

Change your Mind Set

When Damarie walked through the door the lights were dim, he could smell the scent of vanilla and cherry. "J!" He yelled as he walked through the living room, "I'm here in the kitchen." Him and J meet there.

He looked around at the living room, it looked spectacular. "What J, you decided to come home and just go crazy cleaning up?"

"Something like that" J replied.

He walks through the kitchen to the dining room and realized she prepared a candle lit dinner.

She walked out of the kitchen with a big smile on her face, "I figured we should stay in. I'm sure you're tired and you made me feel so special today that I wanted to do something for you baby. So sit down, let me cater to your needs and feed you."

"Thank you babe, cause I am tired, this all looks so nice, and what we eating? Cause it smells bomb."

"Well I made steaks, lobster tails, cream potatoes, and salad."

"Now that is what I'm talking 'bout boo, you know daddy love all dat."

J sat Damarie down and tied his handkerchief around his neck, and brought his plate out to him.

She sat next to him smiling, asking him how everything tasted. He never responded he just kept eating. She thought "that's a good sign, I guess" as she laughed to herself. As he neared the end of his meal, he began to talk to J about some of his upcoming plans.

"Boo, I was thinking you already work for a mortgage company as loan officer, have you ever thought about being a realtor?"

"No not really, it's a lot of work."

"But you could make bank doing it if you sell in profitable areas. I think you need to take a few classes and get your license and do it. I'm also thinking we have too many expenses right now to have a baby and get

Kahladee

married so if we're going to do it, we need to scale back, cut cost, and make better choices."

"Like what Damarie?"

"For instance, our rental properties. How much are we actually generating in cash?"

" Not much babe, we pretty much break even."

" So whose lease is up soon and who has been late more than three times this year?"

The Williams family lease is up in two months, and they have been late on several occasions." J answered.

"Ok then J, we won't renew their lease, let them know tomorrow."

"J, we're going to move in that house, you can make a few renovations to freshen it up, pay to break your lease on your place. Immediately put your stuff in storage until our move is final, also call Raneka ask her if she and Ja'Lee want to move into our other rental property.

J, excited to hear him making plans about a baby and marriage so she tried to support him and said "the lease on the other house is up in three months, and if I'm not mistaken, the Hutchins really want us to sell it to them baby, they love that house."

"Well get your license and sell it to them, so we can make a profit and get on all of this right away."

"And what are you going to do with this place?" J asked sarcastically.

"Well if you must know, I'm going to let one of my block boys move in."

"Oh really and who is that?" J asked.

"Not sure yet. But don't worry about it babe. I just want you to focus on the fact that we're moving in together," then he playfully kissed her and said "you're about to be your own boss and trust me this is going to beneficial for the both of us in the long run."

J got up from the table rolling her eyes.

"What is wrong with you J?"

"Nothing, it just seems like you making many decisions without asking me my opinion Damarie."

"Don't look at it like that J, you said you want to be married, have a family, and stop side hustling right?"

"Yes for the 100th time I said it!"

"Ok. Then let me get us to that point."

She started to walk off still with an attitude.

"Where you going, J?"

"To take out the trash."

"Since when do you take out trash J?"

Kahladee

"Since now, I'm being treated like trash so I may as well assemble the position."

Damarie stood up and went after her getting in her face and snatching the bag from her hand. He looked at her with a don't fuck with me look and walked out the door to take it out, on the way down to the chute he could see take out boxes through the bag.

"I knew her ass didn't cook that food; she didn't have time to clean up like that, and make it all sensual." All he could do was laugh because he respected her gangster, one thing stood out in his mind. "How the fuck was she going to be a mother, if she didn't really want to cook for two let alone for four or five?"

He headed back down the hall to the apartment when he opened the door. J was standing there crying, with her Coach duffle bag and make up case packed. He walked by looking down at her shaking his head "now what Ma?"

"Nothing, I'm going home to my place."

"Fine J, go home and cool off because you really on one right now. I don't know which one, but you definitely on something."

"Call me when you get there so I know you made it home safe, please." He kissed her on the cheek and let her out the door.

Damarie headed to the dining room and kitchen to clean up and blow out the candles. He showered and kicked back on his black leather sectional to watch TV and get caught up on sports.

After an hour had passed, he saw J hadn't called like he asked her to, so he picked up the phone and called her. It rang twice and went to voicemail. He mumbled "she get on my last nerve, spoiled ass brat." Moments later, he got a text from J; it read "I'm home, not that you really give a fuck because if you cared you would not have let me leave."

He responded to her "Baby, take some Midol and go to bed it's obvious your hormones are out of balance, I love you good night." She text him back with "Fuck off."

The next morning Damarie woke up on the couch with J standing over him. He looked up at her, startled.

She smiled and said "Couldn't sleep in the bed without me huh?"

"No Ma, I fell asleep on the couch as you can tell." "Aren't you supposed to be at work, J?"

" I called in, to start taking care of this long to do list you asked me to take care of Damarie."

He rose off the couch, sat up, turned off the TV and headed back to the bedroom; he peeled the comforter back and got in the bed. J followed behind him nagging, "What Damarie, you going to sleep the day away?"

Kahladee

No, I am going to sleep my headache off then get up and handle business J."

"Call me and wake me up at noon please Ma. I really don't feel good right now."

"As you wish," she replied and headed out to the living room to make calls and set up meetings regarding all the property matters.

Chapter 8

The Move

A month later, all of Damarie's plans were coming into place. J started classes for her realtor license. Instead of giving the Williams proper notice like he asked her to she secretly paid them to move out early so she could have the place renovated the way she wanted to. Even though Damarie told her to make generous changes she took it upon herself to have more done than necessary.

When Damarie asked why they were so much over budget, she lied to him by saying the Williams had moved out without notice and gutted the place of the all the appliances, right down to the copper. He questioned why she had not told him and she said she did not want him to stress and worry and that she had filed an unlawful detainer on them and reported them to police. Damarie told her he appreciated her being strong and handling business.

With it being only two weeks until they moved in together, J decided to do some more shopping for the house. She and Damarie had plenty of things that would go with the decor but she wanted a few new pieces so she enlisted her best shopping partner, Raneka. J mainly wanted to brag and shortly a few pieces turned into twenty thousand dollars' worth of new furniture. She ended up furnishing the whole house and only kept a few of her own pieces, giving everything else to her mother. With J in class and busy renovating, Damarie had a lot of time to reconstruct his game and prepare to go international. He planned on telling "Work" on his next trip to New Jersey that he had built his team even though he was still looking for a female to take J's place.

Mega had proven himself to be a self-made hustler. He had the North side on lock and had built clientele up the ass. Damarie really felt he could trust him so he asked him to take over the lease to his apartment and guard the product.

Mega accepted Damarie's offer without hesitation. He had recently broken up with his baby's mom and was back on his mother's couch. He had enough money to get his own place but deep down he hoped that he and his girl would work things out and she would ask him home but that didn't happen, so like any man he started to live a bachelor's life and Damarie's place was the proper place to begin. It had plasma TVs, a leather sectional and much more it was a true man cave. He couldn't wait to move in.

Two weeks flew by so fast. J wanted to hire movers but Damarie told her he would just get the block boys to do it so she rented a truck and had them meet her at the storage unit.

When they arrived at the storage unit, there were tons of boxes and TVS, but no furniture. Damarie was puzzled and asked "where's all your stuff?"

She answered by telling him she had a surprised for him, he looked upset but because the fellas were around he played it off with a smirk.

Once all the boxes were on the truck he asked Mega and Ja'Lee to follow them to the new crib. "He jumped in the car with J, and asked so "What's the surprise? You already had your stuff moved?"

"You will see in due time baby just chill," she answered. It was about a thirty minute drive from the city to the burbs.

Damarie said nothing to J the whole way there. Deep down he knew there was no surprise but some deep spending had went down. Once at the house J got out the car and went to the truck where Mega and Ja'Lee. She asked them to wait a few minutes before they started unloading so she could give Damarie his surprise.

Damarie was standing at the door looking very annoyed telling J to hurry up. She ran over with the key and

Kahladee

opened the door. He walked in and smelled the fresh paint. He loved the colors she had chosen but when he saw the furniture was not from J's apartment he was pissed off. He turned and asked her "where the fuck all this shit come from? She responded "baby, don't you like it? He spat back "it's not if I like it, it's about we didn't discuss this." He walked from room to room everything was new he grew madder by the second and "all these renovations what the fuck... I told you we need to scale down, what the fuck were you thinking about?"

"Baby, I'm sorry I thought I was doing a good thing; I wanted to make you happy."

"Well, I'm not so I hope damn well you are. How much did all this shit cost?" She told him with the renovations everything was fifty thousand dollars.

He went bananas yelling at her..."Take this shit back, call them motherfuckers and tell them to come and get all this shit now!"

"Damarie calm down, I can't take it back."

"Why not J? Because baby I gave all my stuff to my mom. She told me she needed furniture so rather than buying her all new stuff, I gave her mine. She's been having money problems baby so I have been helping her."

Damarie looked her dead in the face and told her, "Don't spend another dime without my approval. Do you understand me?"

"Yes baby I'm sorry," she started crying and walked away.

Around that time Ja'Lee rang the bell because he could hear Damarie outside. Damarie open the door, "I'm sorry man, let's get this shit in here so I can bounce I don't even want to look at her right now."

Mega came in with the first box damn near screaming, "Damn Damarie you doing big like a mutha fucka! This shit raw as hell bro I'm not mad at you my nigga." Ja'Lee looked at Mega with not a good time face. Mega took heed and ran out to grab more boxes.

They finished bringing the last of the boxes in. J had them marked by room so it went fast. She stayed out of sight unless Damarie asked her to do something. She knew she had pushed the wrong buttons.

Before the fellas left, Damarie called J and asked her for the key to his old place so he could give it to Mega. J grabbed her purse off the counter and started looking for the key, "I can't find it," J said with a stiff look, "I must have dropped it or lost it somewhere I'm sorry."

Damarie looked at her and said "you know J you are sorry a lot these days." He turned around and headed out the door Ja'Lee and Mega followed like two kids.

Once she heard them drive off, she went through her purse and took the key out and put it under the living room vent.

They took the U-Haul back and Damarie offered to buy the guys dinner for helping out, they both declined his offer they could tell he wasn't in the social mood so they went back to Damarie's old apartment which was now Mega's. Damarie gave Mega the run down about keeping low traffic and who the neighbors were and told him if any one asked him, he was to tell them they were brothers.

He told Mega since he had all new furniture that he could have all his old stuff, Mega offered to pay for it but Damarie told him just to stay loyal and that would be payment enough. As far as the keys went, they all needed a copy. Mega was fine with it, he just told them to make sure they called first just in case he had a female he was entertaining.

Ja'Lee's phone rang, he answered, and it was Raneka. "Hey Ja' Lee what's up?"

"Nothing Raneka what you need?'

"Nothing, J just called me crying saying Damarie was mad at her so I'm going to drive over help unpack and just talk to her."

"That's fine just stay out they business is all I ask."

About a week had passed since Damarie blew up on J about spending so much money without his consent; he was over it and started to forgive her. She stayed out of his way for the most part just to allow him time to cool off. She had everything unpacked in order; the house really looked good. He had to give it to her she had a good eye for fashion and décor, but he also knew he had to watch her spending habits.

Damarie's trip to New Jersey was coming up in a couple of days, he was debating if he would have J ride with him, but decided against it because he didn't want her to think he was trying to ease her back in the game.

He was lounging around the house when he all of sudden got a text message. He picked up his phone and the message read "Hey stranger." He texted back "Who dis?" A response came through, it read, "What you got amnesia." He started laughing and texted back, "I didn't notice you without your work suit." he was hit back with, "lol."

He then picked up the phone and dialed Dameta. She answered on the first ring, "What's up?" He replied, "Not much here."

"What about you, now days?"

"Not much at all. I'm actually bored, and wondered if you wanted to go grab a drink or something?"

 "Yeah Dameta, I would like that when, where, and what time?"

She answered, "How about now?"

"That's cool; let's go to Chauncey's. I will meet you there in thirty minutes."

Dameta got there first and asked to be seated near the back where it was quiet. But quiet wasn't her only reason

Kahladee

for wanting to sit in the back, it was also where she could see the door.

When he walked in she stood up and waved him over to her table, he walked up and gave her a friendly hug. "So how's life and that job treating you?"

" Life is good, but the job on the other hand is no longer."

"Really, what happened?"

"Well they passed me up for partner again so I quit."

"Good for you. Are you going to be ok financially?"

"Actually I'm cool. I'm not a big spender. And to be honest, I could not work for five years and be ok."

"Well that's good."

"So what are you going to do with yourself with all this time off?"

"Well I figure I will take a few overdue vacations, spend some time with my grandma, and catch up with friends. So what about you Damarie any new business ventures as we discussed?"

"Actually I have had made a few changes with your advice of course."

"Well that's good, I'm glad to see I made a difference in your thinking."

Damarie was looking at Dameta thinking she's, intelligent, pretty, soft spoken, and kind. He wondered if she would be a good candidate for J's old spot, no one would ever suspect her, she's a lawyer. It wouldn't hurt to ask, all she could say was no... What the hell? he thought. "Dameta I have question for you, but I don't want you to think less of me when I ask you this."

"Well hit me, Damarie."

"Ok," he began, "What do you think about joining my team?"

"What! Did I hear you right?"

"Yes you did."

"Are you serious?"

"Yes. I see potential in you. You know the law, you are smart, and no one would ever suspect you."

"So what would joining your team entail for me?"

"Well going out of town, local and international, making cash and product drops."

She interrupted him, "So you are asking me to sell drugs?"

"Yes I am," he answered her point blank.

Kahladee

She started to laugh so hard the waiter had to come over and ask her to quiet down.

"Look Dameta, I don't expect you to have an answer right now, take a couple of days and really think about it before you completely blow off the idea."

She looked at him speechless before she answered, "OK, I will think about and get back to you."

They ordered drinks and talked about each other's goals for the future.

Damarie insisted on paying the tab even though she invited him out. He hugged her good bye and told her to get back to him in a couple days before he went out of town. She politely told him "I will call you no matter what the answer."

That night Dameta went home thinking about Damarie's offer she thought "this is nuts, I'm educated, financially stable, and really a white-collar woman not a white collar criminal." However, she also thought about the potential for excitement. She had never done anything daring in her life.

Several days went past as she thought long and hard about the pros and cons of the opportunity. There were really no pros just cons for her. On her fourth day of thinking, she decided she would call him back, but she was so shy about the matter she decided to send him a text instead.

He had begun to give up on her responding to him in fact he thought he scared her away when all of sudden he got text from her that read "Count me in." He jumped off the couch with excitement; J ran in the living room and asked "What are you jumping up and down for baby?"

"It's nothing, just something I been working on finally came together" he responded.

Damarie dialed Ja'Lee to let him know he found a female and that he would need him to come to New Jersey on the next run and he would give him details then. He left the house next in order to call Dameta. She answered again on the first ring, he immediately asked, "Are you sure?" She told him she was sure and said "Let's do it." He told her welcome to the team and let her know he would give her details when he came back into town.

In the meantime, "Dameta, I am giving you a nickname."

"Oh yeah, and what would that be?"

"I'm going to call you Ryde from here on out, if that's cool with you."

"Fine by me."

"I will see you later, Ryde."

"Bye Damarie."

Chapter 9

International Hustlers

Damarie had his team ready, his mind, and home was in order. He was ready to get down to business. He had not spoken to "Work" since the last time he was in New Jersey so this would be good news to "Work." Ja'Lee and Damarie decided that it would be a good idea for him to stay over that Friday night since they had to get up early to head to Jersey.

Raneka didn't have anything to do, so she decided she would stay along with him. J was excited that someone was going to put the guest room to use. While the guys were out on the block, J and Raneka just hung out around the house making homemade pizza and sipping Mosacato. They decided they would have a girl's day that

Saturday. Raneka was all for it. "Let's get our hair, nails, and feet done and do some shopping."

J replied, "Then after all that, we can go out to dinner and hit up a club, it has been a minute for me, what about you?"

"Girl," Raneka replied, "it has been over six months for me, I am game."

It was around midnight and the guys still had not made it in, both of them were used to the guys coming home in the early am.

Raneka told J, "I am lucky if Ja'Lee makes it home by 3am most nights, but I trust him. He has never given me a reason not to."

"Yeah, I trust Damarie too; we vowed never to cheat on one another. I know he is careful on the streets, but I still worry about him. Every time I tell him he needs to get out of the game he gets pissed off and then we don't talk for days. He is extremely agitated with me these days so I try to stay out of his way."

"I feel you, J; you just have to let men do what they do." Just as J, was going to respond she heard a key opening the door. Damarie walked in and Ja'Lee followed, "What's up ladies?" Ja'Lee asked.

"Nothing, just chilling bout to call it a night," J replied. J stood up, "I will go get the guest room ready for you guys." She headed up the stairs, truth be told it was already

Kahladee

ready; she just wanted to make sure they had enough towels and toiletries.

Once she surveyed the room, she headed back down the stairs; they all stood around and talked for a few minutes before everyone headed up to bed. When they got to their bedroom Damarie striped down to his boxers, and headed for their shower, J asked if she could join him. He told her, "Baby, I'm tired as hell and you know I got to roll out in few hours."

"Ok baby, I will take a rain check." J said.

As soon as he got into the shower, she checked his pockets, wallet, and went through his phone. She found nothing suspicious, but still he never turned her down before so she felt really insecure. She also felt so detached from him lately; she started to wonder if she had put too much pressure on him with all this family talk.

She heard him turn the water off, so she quick turned on the TV, threw on his T-shirt, and hopped in bed. Damarie came out with his towel wrapped around his waist, still dripping wet. All J could do was stare at him, she knew she had one damn good man, and she'd better hold onto him or someone else would.

The next morning rolled around so fast Damarie woke up like he had not even been to sleep. He sprung out of bed, called Ja'Lee on his cell phone, Ja'Lee picked up, "Man, why you calling me like I'm not down the hall from you?"

"Because you might be getting some morning love, I didn't want to interrupt." Damarie said.

"Man you crazy as hell because you still would be interrupting..."

"Shut up fool," Damarie chuckled. "Ja' let's be out in 15 minutes."

Damarie hung up the phone and headed for the bathroom to brush his teeth and wash up. He splashed on some Creed cologne, ran some pomade through his 360 waves, threw on a white tee, dark wash Levy's, and to complete his look a Louis Vuitton belt, and sneakers.

J was knocked out cold. He didn't want to wake her so he closed the door quietly behind him on his way out. Ja'Lee was strolling out at the same time dressed in a black tee, Girbaud jeans, and black Prada sneakers. They exited quietly down the stairs.

Damarie tossed Ja'Lee the keys to the truck once they were outside

"Oh you taking full advantage of this huh?" Ja'Lee asked.

"Damn straight, you know J's lazy ass never drives when we make a run."

They headed out the driveway and hit a drive thru for breakfast and they were on their way. They were about an hour into the drive, when Ja'Lee asked, "So are you going to fill me in on our new Block chick or what?"

Kahladee

"Well, I don't know if I would classify her as a block chic." Damarie said.

"Really, what would you call her then?" Ja'Lee asked.

"She is more of a corporate chic; she is educated, sophisticated, and well spoken. Point being nobody will ever suspect her."

"So, just how corporate is she Damarie?"

"She is a lawyer bro."

"What? Are you crazy nigga or are you fucking this bitch?"

"Hell no, I'm not crazy and you know damn well I'm not fucking around on J. Her name is Dameta but she likes to be called Ryde. Trust me on this one bro, she is a true gritter.

"Ryde huh? Sound like some fucking going on to me."

"Shut up hater. She is good looking as hell, true enough, but she's off limits to all of us. She is one of us now, so we are going to respect her, and protect her, bottom line. We have to teach her the ropes as far as the block is concerned, but for the most part she only going to make international moves. All this is going to work out smooth, we'll do a few runs internationally, and we out. That's why we need Mega; he'll hold the block down.

"You right Damarie he is doing the damn thing now. His bird feeder ass baby mom is trying to slide back around, I told him don't fall for her ass because she sees the money, not him."

They bumped the music and smoked blueberry Kush out the truck, the rest of the way. By the time they got there, they were high as hell, hungry, and paranoid. They were both looking for the diccs at every light or corner they hit. Ja'Lee pulled up to the gate at "Works" crib, he looked at Damarie, and "Here we are. Let's do it, bro."

Damarie got out the car dusting the blunt residue off his shirt; they proceeded to walk up to the door, but before they could even knock the maid open the door and walked them back to "Works" office. "Work" stood up and asked with a slight grin on his face, "And to what do I have the pleasure of doing for my favorite customers?"

Damarie didn't hesitate to answer, "Well last month, you told me you were ready for a new venture, and here I am a month later with my business partner ready to get down to business."

"Ahh did you say ready to get down to business or talk business?" "Work" replied.

"You heard me right, let's get down to business."

"Ok then, here's is my pitch," "Work" stated while walking around to shut his office door, "I told you I wanted to make international moves, and I came up with a grand plan to do so. As you already know, I work for my father in-law, and he has many companies. However, "Work" lowered his voice, "I don't want to work for him or be married to his spoiled ass daughter any longer. But I have also come accustomed to a certain type of lifestyle as you can see. The problem is I can't keep it if I leave her, not because I don't have my own money but because even though she doesn't need it, she would take me for every penny.

With that said, here is my plan. We own three sugar companies internationally one in, Spain, Indonesia, and the Dominican Republic. Out of the three, I have narrowed down the Dominican Republic to be the easiest to smuggle dope from, simply because it's only an hour and 45 minute flight. We will only need to make three trips there to become self-made millionaires.

I have three workers that work at the sugar plant that will stuff the sugar boxes with coke; each box can hold one bird. Every run made, 100 birds will be shipped back to Jersey; and dropped off at the family's storage facility. In addition, the product will flood the streets as usual and we will sell it for more because it's pure, nothing synthetic about it. And the beauty of it all … we get the product cheaper because of the large quantity."

Ja'Lee spoke up and said to "Work," "You" seem to have this all figured out. Let me make sure I understand, so we only make the cash drops and the rest is up to your shippers? That sounds easy enough; it's just a lot of cash to travel with."

"Exactly Lee, now you with me, I will have you pose as FDA workers, get you fake IDs, badges, and more importantly passports. Cash drops will only be made at night when my three recruits work. We'll send a different person on each run, others can go for the sake of support but on different flights and under their real name so that way no connection can be made between any of you." "Work" instructed.

"So Damarie, I assume you have someone else in mind to do one of the runs?

"Yes I do, it's a female, and she's loyal."

"Well good it will take me about a week to get all of your ID's and tools. I will plan on doing this in DC next Thursday; this will save you a trip back to Jersey and give me a chance to meet your other recruit. "Work" said.

"We have talked about everything except where we will stay when we get there. Damarie inquired.

 "Work" replied "we own several timeshares; I will have one set up for each run. If I were you, I would make it a vacation because each timeshare location is a beautiful place."

Damarie got up from his chair; "I think we're done here. We will plan to see you next week "Work." Do you want the usual?"

"No. We are good for this trip, Damarie. I think we will be doing enough business in the upcoming month or two that we better take a break before all the jet lag."

 They all shook hands and headed out. Damarie and Ja'Lee had already planned to stop by and take Damarie's mom out to lunch, as well as hook up with some old friends while they were in New Jersey.

Chapter 10

Up in Da' the Club

Back in DC, J and Raneka started out their day by heading over to Queens Salon, to get their hair done, and catch up on the latest gossip. They both got their usual hair dos and headed out for a manicure and pedicure. After that, they did some shopping and picked out outfits to wear to Club Satin. J picked out a black and nude colored mini- dress, with nude 4 inch heels to match.

Raneka picked out royal blue pencil skirt, with a sheer taxi cab yellow sleeveless blouse, complete with royal blue and yellow stiletto toeless booties. After shopping, they headed back to the crib to eat and rest up before they hit the club.

By the time 9:00 pm rolled around, Raneka and J had eaten and had a few drinks so they were both half ass hammered so instead of resting they pumped up the music and proceeded to get ready.

Since Raneka used to be a makeup artist, she did their makeup staying with the color scheme of their outfits. When she was done she told J "Girl we killing shit." They locked up the house and headed out; Raneka decided she would drive Ja'Lee's Audi A7. They were at the club by 10:30 pm.

Raneka pulled up to the valet, got out and told the driver "Don't scratch my baby" chuckling, but being very serious. J hopped out smiling as if she just hit the red carpet. They headed straight to VIP line. Once in their booth they ordered a bottle of Grey Goose and Moet. They poured themselves a drink and started dancing, the music was jumping.

They decided to walk around to see if they could find some familiar faces. They hit the main floor, it was crowed as hell, and men were trying to holler at every angle. Raneka grabbed J's hand and pulled her on the dance floor "Let's dance bitch," they started dancing to the music when J looked up and saw two of her colleagues from work, Amy and Veronica.

They headed over to speak to J, laughing, they asked her what her stuck up ass was doing here. She also started laughing and told the girl, "I'm trying to kick it just like you." J introduced them to Raneka, and invited them back upstairs to their booth. All four of the ladies polished off both bottles and were having a party of their own, when J's colleagues decided to leave. Raneka told J "I'm still ready to kick it; I'm just ready to leave this spot." J responded, "Shit, let's go across the street to Seduce, the strip club." Raneka said, "What! Are you for real?"

"Hell yeah, I'm for real, from what I hear, they be kickin it over there."

They signaled the server, paid the tab, and headed across the street wobbling and pulling on each other. They were drunk as hell. They walked inside; everybody from the hood was there, mainly niggas but a few hood rats. Raneka and J headed to the bar seated themselves and grabbed some more drinks; J felt a tap on her shoulder.

She turned around and to her surprise, it was Mega. He asked "What y'all doing in here?" she answered sarcastically, "I guess I'm trying to get a dance and a drink". He laughed at her and said "a dance maybe, but from the looks of things neither one of u need another drink." J responded, "So what you going to call our men and tell on us?" "Nah, it's not like that. Just find me before you ladies leave so I can make sure you're all right."

Mega paid for their drinks and headed off toward the champagne room, he figured he owed to himself, he was feeling good, looking good, and he had stepped his game up since his money was right. He had on a pair of True Religion jeans, a white polo, and a pair of Creative recreational shoes. As he approached the champagne room the women standing at the podium, looked up and asked him, "Can I help you sir?"

Kahladee

RYDE

He responded, "As a matter of fact, you can. I was coming over to treat myself to private dance but I see something else has got my full attention."

"And what would that be she asked?"

"That would be you beautiful."

"I believe we have met before," she responded and then she asked, "What did you say your name was?"

"Well I didn't say, but my name is Mega."

"Well Mega, we have met before. It was a few months back at Chauncey's. You sent me and my girl over some drinks and then all hell popped off."

"Now I got you, how are you?"

"I'm good thanks."

"So do you mind telling me your name again?"

"My name is Mija."

"Well Mija, I would like to take you out sometime if that's all right."

She paused and thought to herself he looks completely different compared to the first time I met him. "You know Mega I would like that."

They exchanged numbers and then there was this awkward silence.

Mija spoke up and said, "I manage the champagne room would you still like a dance? I can give it to you at half price." Mega didn't want to seem thirsty, so he declined her offer. He gave her a hug and told her, "You will hear from me real soon."

Mega decided he would check on the girls, when he made his way back out to the main floor, J and Raneka was in a confrontation with the bartender. He hurried up to the bar and asked what the problem was. The bartender responded, "They wanted more drinks and they have clearly had enough, it's time for them to go." Mega grabbed J and Raneka by their hands and told them it was time to go. J started tripping on Mega, "You don't tell us what to do cause Damarie is your boy now. You think you running shit? Let me go now!"

Mega looked at Raneka and tried to rationalize with her since he wasn't getting through to J, "Look Ma, let me call you ladies a cab. I just don't want to see you in trouble."

Raneka responded Mega, "I appreciate your concern but we got dis, we grown as hell, we got this."

Mega made sure they crossed the street safely and called Damarie he didn't get an answer, he then called Ja'Lee no answer. He texted them and told them both to call him A.S.A.P.

That was all he could do for now. However, he did decide to follow them home to make sure they made it safe. He jumped in his navigator and waited for the valet to pull up with their car. Once they were in their car, he followed

Kahladee

them. Raneka was swerving all over the road and he could see them being all animated and acting a fool. Raneka hit the express way pushing the Audi to 70 miles per hour.

Mega could barely keep up in his new Lincoln Navigator, he tried phone J to tell them to slow down but she didn't answer her phone. Raneka kept going full speed Mega was going 75 so Raneka had to be pushing at least 85 coming around a sharp curve, Mega suddenly saw the brake lights of the Audi, the car jerked hard, and started spinning out of control before he knew it, he heard a big crackling sound.

Raneka had crashed straight into the median. He threw his hazards on and pulled behind them. He got out of his truck as fast as he could, running to the driver side of the car. When he got up to the car, he couldn't see that well, nor could he get the door open, it was smashed so bad. He ran over to the passenger side, and opened the door. There was glass everywhere and the air bags had deployed. He could see Raneka sobbing. She appeared to have hit her head. You could tell she was ok, but was sobbing. J kept screaming "my arm hurts."

Mega started yelling at them both, "Get out now! We have to go before the cops get here."

They were both still stupid drunk but shook up nonetheless. Neither one of them were moving so he lifted J out of the car and ran her back to the truck, she kept screaming, "Oh your hurting my arm!" He paid her no mind and put her in the back of his truck.

He hurried over to Raneka next this was challenging cause he was big he had to maneuver the seats to get her banging her up even more. He got her out and ran her back to the car seating her next to J. He ran back to the Audi for a final time, grabbed their purses, and put the hazards on. He got in the truck and told them "I'm taking you both to the hospital , don't answer any questions all you know is somebody hit you and kept going, I was behind you and I saw it and helped you, do you understand me?" They both replied, "Yes." Ja'Lee finally called Mega back asking question after question. What's going on? Is the block cool? Where you at? Mega finally got a chance to respond, "The block's good. Where you guys at?"

"We just got back," Ja' Lee told him, "Look bro; meet me at the county hospital. J and Raneka were in a car accident and I'm taking them to the hospital. They will be fine. I will explain as soon as everything is situated."

 By the time he got them to the hospital they had somewhat sobered up they were both quiet like he told them, but they were both crying.

Mega went to the desk and spoke to the nurse, "Mam, these two ladies have been in a hit and run accident, and need to be looked at." She pushed the clip board back at him and said, 'I'm going to need you to fill out their information for me please."

Kahladee

Mega responded, "Sure thing, ma'am."

Before he could sit down, Raneka started complaining, "My head hurts so bad." She had big goose egg on it and it was bleeding from the center. J started crying about her arm and began to throw up. The nurse called for two wheel chairs, had them seated and hurried to get them a room. She started asking them questions but they both kept crying and saying they were in pain.

There were wheeled backed into rooms next to each other leaving Mega in the waiting are where he continued struggling to fill out their paperwork since he didn't know shit about them. He returned the clipboards and told the clerk that's all he knew. He turned around to take a seat and Damarie and Ja'Lee came running in both speaking at the same time and asking one hundred questions all at once.

"Where are they, are they ok, what the fuck happen, how they end up with you?" Mega put his hands over his mouth motioning for them to be quiet he then walked them to a quiet corner to tell them what happen.

He told them just to flow with the hit and run story otherwise when they left the hospital both their women would be going to jail cause they are both dusted as hell. Damarie asked whose car was they in. Mega answered "The Audi." Ja'Lee looked pissed; he asked "Is it fucked up bad?" Mega replied, "Yeah, from what I could see."

Damarie told Ja'Lee, "It's a just a car. Let's just make sure these two dumb asses are going to be all right and we will work out the kinks later."

They thanked Mega and told him they could take it from here, they shook hands, and Mega left. Damarie and Ja'Lee walked over to the desk and asked for the girls. The clerk gave them each a number and pointed them back to the direction of the rooms.

Raneka was back from X-ray; Ja'Lee ran to her side and told her "Baby you will be alright." She started crying, "I'm so sorry about the car Lee, it all happen so fast." Ja' Lee told her to just chill and not to worry. Her head had been bandaged up from where she was hit. Other than that, she only had bruises and a few small cuts from the glass.

Since J wasn't back from X-rays Damarie popped over to Raneka's room to check on her, she was resting so he didn't say anything to her, Ja'Lee told him, and "We are just waiting on the results, anything from J yet?" "No not yet, she not back from her X-rays."

Damarie walked back to J room pulling the curtain behind him, he sat down thinking to himself, "I don't know what the fuck those two were thinking."

The MD walked in and introduced himself. Damarie stood up and shook his hand and told him his name, "Well Damarie the good news is she will be ok; the bad news is she has three broken ribs and a broken arm. We will need to do surgery on her arm and her ribs will have to heal on their own."

Kahladee

"However, we can't do surgery tonight because her blood alcohol level is extremely high and we will need to flush the alcohol out of her system before we proceed with the surgery on Monday morning." Damarie thanked the Doctor and went to tell Ja'Lee the news.

When he got to Raneka's room, she was being discharged. Ja'Lee told Damarie "She has a concussion but she can go home." Damarie told him "that's good; J has a broken arm and three broken ribs so she is not going home. She has to have surgery on Monday."

Lee just shook his head, "Damn bro, this shit is fucked up right now but we will get through it. I'm going to get her home to rest. I will be back in the morning when I get Raneka settled."

"All right Lee, I will see you later."

By the time J was settled in a room, it was 6am, Sunday morning. Damarie was tired, mad, and just plain agitated about the whole situation. He asked for a blanket and hit the roll out bed hard. About 11 am Damarie woke up and J was still sleep, so he went to the cafeteria grabbed a bite to eat, and headed to the gift shop. He picked out a bear and some flowers for J.

When he got back to the room J was waking up slowly, he just sat and stared at her. She was still pretty as ever even though he was mad at her for being so careless and childish. He walked over to her and kissed her on the forehead and told her that Raneka was fine and everything would be ok. "Are you mad at me, Damarie?"

"No J, I'm just glad you're ok. After your surgery, I'm going to take you home and take care of you."

Ja'Lee walked in the room with flowers in hand. He looked at J and told her, "We can't leave you two alone." She laughed and cried at the same time causeing her ribs hurt.

He walked over to her bed smiled at her told her to rest up for surgery tomorrow. Damarie told J he would be back later he was going home to shower, rest and make some calls, and get things in order so when she did come home things would be ready.

Chapter 11

Put it all in Order

Damarie went home and handled things just as he said he would. He enlisted the help of J's mom Candace, he told her what happen and that he needed her help because he had a lot of business to take care of and he would be in and out of town for the next two months. J's mother stepped right in; she hung up the phone from Damarie, packed a bag and headed over to the house.

Once she got there, she hugged Damarie passed him her bag, and barged right in and started making calls. She called J's boss first, told her the news, and started the leave of absence process. Next, she cleaned the house, it was clear that Raneka and J had a lil' party the night before.

When she was done with that, she cooked a meal, told Damarie to eat and rest because she was heading to the hospital to see her baby. Damarie locked the door and headed up to the bedroom, he fell asleep for about two hours until his phone rung and woke him. He answered it. It was Mega checking up on everything. "We cool, thanks for taking charge and handling things."

"Mega, I want to let you know we have new business venture, a new female teammate, and we need you to handle things on the block by yourself for a while."

"We will meet up on Thursday to discuss details and you can meet our new member."

"That sounds good to me. Just let me know where and what time on Thursday."

They hung up the phone, and Damarie dialed Ryde. She picked up on the third ring and he immediately started talking, "Listen, shit's hectic, but plans are still in place. My girl was in an accident but she will be alright. I need you to meet up with me on Thursday to discuss details and meet the crew."

"Well that's fine with me, until then I wish you the best with everything else."

"Thanks Ryde. Talk to you Thursday."

Ryde hung up the phone with a smile on her face.

Ryde and Mija had been watching TV and when Damarie called her, Mija was staring at her the whole time. Mija sat up and looked at her for a minute before she asked who that was? Dameta responded "Just a friend."

"Well you not smiling like it was just a friend."

"Well it was, nosey woman."

Mija asked her what she was going to do later. "I'm not doing anything what about you?"

"I'm going on a date." Mija replied.

"With who?"

"This guy name is Mega. You actually met him that night we went to Chauncey's."

"Was he the guy who sent us over the drinks?"

"Yeah, he was at the club the other night looking fine as hell, he asked me out. I hesitated at first, but he looks like he has stepped his game up."

"Where you two going?"

"Well we decided we'd meet back up at Chauncey's since that's where we first met. I need you to be my back up plan since you have nothing to do, come out with me and if this me and dis nigga don't hit it off, you can be my excuse to leave. All you have to do is hang out off to yourself for 15 minutes , and when I get up to go to the bathroom you follow and I will let you know if he's cool. He will not even know we came together."

"No, I'm not doing that lame shit.

"Please Dameta. I will buy you something cute."

"Like what a hutchie dress, Mija?"

"Yeah, with leopard print." At that, they both just started laughing.

"Fine I will do it. What time do I need to be there?"

"Come at 8:45; meet me in the ladies room by nine."

Meanwhile back at Ja' Lee and Raneka's place, Ja'Lee was on the phone talking to the insurance company About the accident, the car had been towed and they were sending agent out within the next day so to see if it was repairable .

He got off the phone frustrated but there was nothing he could do about it. He headed back to the bedroom to check on Raneka. He laid next to her and asked if she needed anything. She declined. She actually told him that she didn't have an appetite.

"Lee, I'm really sorry. I don't know what came over me. I had way too much to drink. I was feeling all by myself and just wanted to have a good time. I wish we had listened to Mega."

Kahladee

"Yeah, I wish you would have too," he said angrily, "you could have been killed. You didn't even ask me to drive my car."

"Is that all you care about is the car?"

"No its not I care about you my point is you don't know what I had in the car."

"While you out drunk and popping your collar… If you would listen to somebody other than J, you would not have that Easter egg on your shit right now."

"It is not her fault Lee, its mine. I decided to take the car."

"It doesn't matter. Both of y'all wrong. Your men are out here hustling and taking risks and all you two do is spend money and fuck shit up. Bottom line, when all this shit is over, you going to have to sit your ass down and find some new hobbies cause the ones you adopted is costing paper, time, and tension we don't need. I'm leaving Raneka cause I'm heated right now, call me if you need something."

He walked out the room and headed for the door before he opened he could hear her crying, he started to go back but he started thinking she needed to think about the dumb ass choices she was starting to make. Ja'Lee headed out taking Raneka's' infinity G35 for a drive, "I should crash her shit and see how she like it."

Ja'Lee felt bad for the way he talked to Raneka. He drove around for about a half hour, and decided he would order some take out from Fatties Bistro, to take home to her, he also stopped and picked her up some flowers.

When he returned home, she was in the living room with a cold pack on her head. He sat next to her passing her the flowers and apologizing for his attitude.

Back at Dameta and Mija's, Mija was getting ready for her date with Mega, she was careful not to wear anything too sexy, because she was really digging him. She thought about him all night, and was surprised when he called so fast. This could mean two things, he was really digging her or he was just trying to hit and quit it. She decided to wear a pair of black skinny leg, Deréon jeans, and a black satin Deréon top to match; she picked a pair of basic black stiletto heels.

Dameta walked in the room, "Mija is that you?"

"Yeah it's me, why what is wrong?"

"Nothing, girl. You covered up for a date, oh no he cancelled, I'm so sorry"

"No ass wipe, he didn't cancel I'm not trying to put myself all out there, that's all.

"Well Mija, I am sorry if I offended you, don't get me wrong you are my girl and you look good no matter what you wear. It's just out of character for you."

"Dameta, we good I'm just feeling him and I don't want him to get the wrong idea that's all."

 Dameta put on a pair of jeans and a simple button up too since she was just there as back up. Mija left at eight as planned. Dameta told her, "I will meet you in the rest room at 9pm."

Mija got there first; she sat in the hostess seat toward the front so Mega and Dameta could spot her. Mija ordered a glass of pink Mosacato as she waited patiently for Mega. She was nervous and hoped the wine would ease her mind.

She took out her compact and checked her face for the third time. As she was putting her compact away she heard a voice say to her "put that away because you are beautiful." She looked up and there was Mega standing over her and gave her a dozen of red roses. She said thank you and smiled.

He was looking damn good, a fresh cut and shave, wearing a pair of dark wash jeans and a black button up. He smelled so good, she had to ask what scent he was wearing, and he told he was wearing a classic scent his mother gave him for his birthday, Cool Water.

They hit off right away, he told jokes that made her laugh; they talked about their childhoods, and what paths they were on in life now. He did tell her he had a two-year-old son, but that didn't matter to her.

They put their dinner order in and Mija ordered another glass of wine Mega ordered a straight Hennessey.

Mija looked at her watch it was 9pm she had forgot to meet Dameta in the rest room she asked him to excuse her, and she headed toward the ladies room. Dameta was sitting on the bench outside the restroom with a smirk on her face.

"Dameta, I am so sorry! I was caught up in the moment and I didn't even see you when you came in."

"Did you see him?"

"Yes I did, he looks handsome."

"Well it looks like you are enjoying each other, chic so I am going to getting out of here."

"Thank you for your support, Dameta. I got a good feeling about him."

"Good now get back to your date you can fill me in later see you at home tonight."

Mija replied, "Maybe."

Dameta told her "You had better come home, fool."

Mija laughed and hurried back to Mega, just in time because their food had arrived. They ate and talked awhile longer before saying their goodbyes Mega offered to drop Mija off, but she insisted to walk the four blocks.

Kahladee

He hugged her and kissed her goodbye and told her he would call her soon. Mija walked about two blocks when she heard her phone ring, it was Mega.

"Hello"

"Hey, beautiful."

"Hey, what's up?"

"Nothing, I said I would call you soon."

She started laughing, but he could tell she was glowing through the phone. "Good night, Mija take special care." She just smiled and hung up.

Chapter 12

Get Life in Order

The following Monday came and Damarie and J's mother Candace headed down to the hospital for J's surgery. They saw her for 15 min before they wheeled her down to surgery. Damarie kissed her and told her that he loved her. Her mother did the same. The surgery took a total of three hours from start to recovery.

She came through just fine. They kept her until the following Tuesday, they wanted to make sure she was not dehydrated, and did not develop pneumonia from her rib fractures.

Damarie sent her mother home until Thursday so he could spend time with J before he started going out of town. He did not tell J his plans of leaving because he did not want to argue, he also failed to warn her that he had a new female working for him.

By the time Thursday rolled around J was feeling a little better. Damarie called Candace to sit with J so he could round up the team and meet up with "Work". He called everyone and told them to meet him downtown at the Hyatt in an hour, also reminding Ja'Lee and Ryde not to forget bring a picture for their fake Ids.

Ryde arrived first; she made eye contact with Damarie and walked toward the waiting area, Ja'Lee and Mega rolled up at the same time. Damarie introduced the fellas to Ryde. Ryde recognized Mega's face but failed to say anything, He realized she looked familiar too but could not pin point from where.

Damarie reiterated everyone's position so there would be no confusion about who was doing what and when. Mega was excited he had to cover all the blocks on his own for about two months. He was eager and willing.

They headed up to the fifth floor where they were meeting "Work;" to Damarie's surprise "Work" had his three recruits with him, along with the ID and Passport machine. "Work" introduced the two Dominican guys as Hector, Ruben, and there was an albino Dominican he called "Paper." Damarie introduced "Work" to Mega and Ryde; they all made small talk while Hector took their pictures and made their Passports, IDs and work badge's.

"Work" could not keep his eyes off Ryde. Damarie noticed this right away; he did not appreciate at it all. "Work" cleared his throat and looked at Ryde; she glanced at him back; asking if there was a problem. He said, "Yes. As a matter a fact there is."

"And what would that be?" Damarie asked.

"Well for starters, she is beautiful but you didn't tell me she was part Dominican."

"I did not think it would matter."

"Work" shot back, "It doesn't. But we need her to have a little more of an edgy look."

Ryde politely asked "Edgy, as far as what"

"Work" replied "I mean as far as sex appeal, I need you to be a sexy business type."

Ryde shot back, "Look, we are dealing coke, not ass here."

"Well she is feisty, Damarie, I like that."

Damarie told "Work," "We will be ready by Monday when we leave, don't worry."

"Work" passed them their plane tickets, and told Damarie he would make the first drop, Ja'Lee and Ryde would be on separate flights. Hector passed them their identification. "Work" passed Damarie the cash in a large duffle. And just like that, the meeting was over.

Kahladee

Afterwards, everyone went their separate ways and Damarie pulled Ryde to the side and apologized for "Work's" comments. He also told her "Work" did not mean anything by it and that he wanted her to look as sophisticated as she truly was.

"Look Damarie; do not worry about me I will be ready Monday just as you told him." Ryde headed home, when she got there Mija had the music up in her room but not as loud as she normally would have, her bedroom door was shut So Dameta headed down the hall to Mija's room. She knocked on the door and Mija told her to come in, she walked in and came straight out and asked Mija to take her shopping because she needed a new look. Mija excitedly asked, "What brings this on?"

"Nothing really. I just need a change," Dameta said, "Hurry up, Mija before I change my mind."

They eagerly headed to the mall; they started in BeBe, Victoria's Secret, Black and White House Market, and too many others to name. Then they headed to purchase purses, accessories, and shoes.

Normally Dameta opted for things all low key. Mija made sure she had things of all colors, she picked out several coach bags, one Gucci bag with two pair of Gucci shoes, and lastly she bought a Louis Vuitton speedy bag.

Mija also took Dameta to have her make up done at the Mac counter and Dameta bought several products. By the time their spree was over Dameta had spent well over ten thousand dollars.

The following Friday, Dameta got up and dressed and headed to the Dominican hair salon to get her hair done. When she got there, she told her stylist that she needed a change, and wanted to cut her hair. She had her hair cut into an introverted bob.

When she left, she felt like a new woman. She went home and went straight to her room, pulled out her luggage and started to pack for her trip on Monday. She was only going to be away three days, she packed sun dresses, flip-flops, heels, shorts, and tank tops, and two business wear outfits, just in case. Next, she packed her toiletries and cosmetics. She was more than ready to go.

She heard Mija coming down the hall, so she came out of her room and paused in the hall. Mija asked her "Who are you and where is my girl?"

Dameta replied, "it is a new me, do you like my hair cut?"

Mija screamed, "No! I love it." They headed out to the living room to talk.

Dameta told Mija, she was going out of town for business and some pleasure if she could find some. Mija just sat and listened.

"So when are you coming back?" Mija asked.

"I will be back Wednesday night, so you will have the house all to yourself enjoy."

Kahladee

Back at Damarie's, Damarie finally told J he was going out of town for a few days. Her ribs and arm may have been broke but her mouth was not. She started in with her questions, "When were you going to tell me? Who are you going with? Are you just going to leave me here alone?" He shut her down with the quickness, "Have I been leaving you alone, J?"

"No let me answer for myself not even to go to the store. As a matter of fact your mom will be staying with until I get back, Raneka will also be here so she can keep an eye on both you since neither one of you can be trusted."

J spat back, "First of all, I'm a grown woman. I don't need no babysitter. Second of all, it's not my mom's responsibility to take care of me it's yours. You are my man."

"Is that a fact J? Because I can't take care of you when you are out busy getting drunk, spending money, running up medical bills, crashing cars, and planning on having a baby. Somebody got to pay for all this shit and it obviously can't be you because you wanted out of the game so you could reap financial havoc upon me. And do me a favor J stop with all the questions! Your mom and Raneka will be here on Sunday Ja'Lee and I will be leaving on Monday morning returning Wed night, so just chill and lets enjoy the rest of the weekend together."

Chapter 13

The First Drop

It was Sunday and Damarie was busy lining things up for the trip, he packed his bag, went grocery shopping for the house, left a thousand dollars in an envelope for Candace just in case they ran into any problems. Later on that evening Ja'Lee and Raneka arrived J was excited since she had not seen Raneka since the accident. They hugged each other and smiled, even though there girls night out had been a tragedy they still had a good time prior to the accident.

Candace arrived by 6pm that evening and just took over. She started cooking and telling everyone what to do. A couple hours after Candace arrived; they all sat down together and ate in the dining room that had never been used. Dinner was fantastic. Candace made Lasagna, salad, and bread sticks. After dinner, she started cleaning up, while the couples played dominoes. It was good to see them all having a good time.

Candace came in and told them it was time to call it a night. They all looked at her like a deer in headlights. She looked back at them, "I'm seriously as hell, you men have a trip to take and you ladies have recovering to do."

Candace asked Damarie if he wanted her to help J with her bath, he told her he would take care of it. Raneka and Ja'Lee headed down to the guest room feeling like two troubled kids. "Goodnight everyone and no hanky panky. All that does is slow down the healing." J shouted at her mom, "Enough already, mother!"

Damarie was awaken by his alarm the next morning at 6am. He shut it off and jumped up like it was the first day of school. He got dressed, grabbed his bags and called Ja'Lee to make sure he was up. He was up and already downstairs waiting.

Before he left the room Damarie kissed J on the lips. She was still asleep; he also left her a gift on his pillow with a letter that read "Open me when you wake up. Love Damarie."

Damarie and Ja'Lee headed out to pick up "Ryde." They arrived at "Ryde's" loft in 15 minutes. Damarie called her on the phone and instructed her to come outside. She had been up for the last two hours so she was more than ready. She put her purse on her arm and grabbed her large Coach duffle exiting quietly so she would not wake Mija.

She walked out of the building and looked for Damarie but she did not see so she called him. "What's up?" he answered, "You need help bringing down your bags?"

"No I got them and I am standing outside, but I don't see you."

He responded, "I don't see you either."

She stuck her hand out and started waving.

"Oh, is that you in the tan and black?" Damarie asked.

"Yeah it is me." He pulled the truck closer while rolling down the window looking her up and down, "I'm sorry, I didn't recognize you. You cut your hair, it looks nice."

"Thank you." She replied.

Ryde was wearing a tan one shoulder top, a pair of black knee length leggings, and gladiator sandals.

Damarie had to side punch Lee, he was starring so hard. Damarie got out and ran around to grab her bag. Ja'Lee got out the car offering her the front seat mainly so he could sneak a peek at her ass. She got in the front, Ja'Lee walked around to the driver's side whispering to Damarie.

"She thick as hell bro."

Damarie rolled his eyes at him, "Get yo ass back in the truck so we can go fool."

It was a good thing they rolled out two hours earlier than was needed because the freeway was packed tight with traffic. Ryde had already fallen asleep an hour into the trip. Ja'Lee was watching a movie.

Damarie was deep in his thoughts, he thought about all the promises he had made to J about starting a family and deep down he was beginning to feel like she was no longer the one for him, her attitude, and behavior was starting to be a major turn off to him. He made a vow to himself that when these trips were over, he was going to have a deeper look inside her heart. He could see the change in her and it wasn't for the better.

He also felt like he had been betrayed by her lately. How could she want out when they hadn't made it to the top? She had become too comfortable, controlling, and most of all he felt that she had become dishonest with him even though he couldn't pin point why.

Ja'Lee could tell something was on Damarie's mind so he just asked, "Are you ok bro?"

"Yeah I'm ok, just tired I guess."

"I know we are only an hour away, but do you want me to drive?"

"Yeah I will get off at the next exit and you can take over."

Damarie pulled into a gas station; he decided he would go inside the store and grab something to munch on. When he walked in, he thought he heard someone call his name. "Hey, it's me over here, Mr. Williams, your past tenant." Damarie made eye contact with him thinking "the nerve of this motherfucker who done stole all my shit and speaking like we're cool?"

Damarie went up to the counter and before he could say anything Mr. Williams started asking questions about J and when the baby was due. Damarie looked confused but he kept listening.

"When J came over offering to pay us out of the lease early because you guys needed to renovate the home and move in because she was expecting it was bittersweet because we loved that home and had just overcame all the problems with the rent. However, when she said we could have all the appliances and she would still pay us, our minds were at ease. That was so nice of you guys we could not have asked for better landlords, even though mistakes with our rent money had been made in the past. J was apologetic that our checks kept getting double cashed, I guess that's why you guys decided to throw in the appliances huh? She even suggested that we move out this way. She sure is a smart woman."

Damarie was boiling, all he could say to Mr. Williams was "I'm glad we could make it up to you and thanks for understanding." He turned and walked out the store.

"Hey Damarie, were you going to buy something?" Mr. Williams asked.

"No, I'm good, take care." He was too pissed to do anything. He thought, "I'm not going to say shit about this to J. I'm going to see how she wiggles her way out of this one."

He got in the back seat of the truck and told Ja'Lee "we got to really talk later man."

The hour flew by and they arrived in NJ. Damarie's flight was in three hours and Ja'Lee and "Ryde's was in four.

Damarie texted "Work" to let him know that everything was on schedule and they were heading into the airport. Damarie made sure he secured the cash well in his carry on. He wrapped it and disguised it in books; he paid the hefty fee of pre-checking his bag that way he would only have to stand in one line.

When he got to the checkpoint to have his carry on tossed through the x-ray conveyor, he got nervous, if he was caught with this kind of money, there would be no explaining, he was going straight to prison.

He walked through the security checkpoint with no problem, now all he had to do was stand at the end of the machine and pray that his bag would come through. Damarie started putting his shoes on, trying to be seemingly regular, rather than just standing there.

By the time he had his shoes on, out came the bag. He had a sigh of relief from within. He headed down to the gate feeling as if he had just accomplished the world's biggest heist.

Once at the gate, he texted "Work" letting him know that he made it through just fine. Next his text to Ja'Lee simply read "I made it, see you both later."

Meanwhile, Ja'Lee and "Ryde," had checked in and decided to grab a bite to eat since their flight was leaving an hour after Damarie's. They spent their time getting to know each other. Ja'Lee found Ryde more laid back than he expected; He could now see what Damarie saw in her, she was more like the sister or friend that you could tell anything to without being judged.

Chapter 14

Touched Down

Damarie landed, claimed his luggage and called "Work" to let him know he had made it. "Work" was excited, "How was the flight?"

"It was good."

"Well, that's good news."

"Where are you right now?"

"I just grabbed my bags."

"Ok that's good. "Paper" the Albino should be outside waiting for you. He will be driving a navy blue Mercedes. I sent him because you can't miss him."

"Work" started laughing and Damarie went along with it even though he wasn't in the laughing mood.

"He will take you to my family's timeshare located on the beach and don't worry about anything, it will be like a mini vacation from here."

Damarie headed outside to look for "Paper," and there he was waiting. He signaled for Damarie to come over to the car. He walked slow but steady, he wanted "Paper" to know that he was his own man and didn't take orders. He got in the car. "Paper" said to him loudly, "Welcome to sheer beauty my friend." "Paper" drove off smiling.

"Paper" gave Damarie a little tour. Once outside, Damarie could see why "Paper" called it sheer beauty. It was indeed beautiful, the trees, the air, everything about it was magnificent in the Dominican Republic. He showed him where the best food was, the sugar plant, souvenir shops, and where he could have some female entertainment, if that was his thing.

"Paper" pulled up to the condo, it was not your ordinary condo, it was on the lower level and was decked out so tight nothing would ever be loose.

When they walked in Damarie was greeted by a maid, she showed him to his room so he could put his things down, and he looked around as he followed her. It had four bedrooms, five baths, a huge kitchen with granite counter tops, and a private pool.

Damarie could not understand why "Work" would ever want to leave such a luxurious life. Damarie put his things

Kahladee

down and headed back out to talk to "Paper." Damarie took a seat on the white leather Natuzzi sectional, "Paper" started giving him the run down; "Esmeralda the maid will be here twenty-four hours a day, she will do your cooking, cleaning, laundry, and if you need or want to go anywhere, she will arrange your transportation. You will make the drop tomorrow night at 10pm during the shift change. I have arranged for the company van to pick you up; you will need to bring your badge and wear the white lab coat that has been provided for you, it is hanging in your closet. You will need to walk around the plant and pose like you are from the FDA for about an hour as you discussed with "Work." I will leave you to rest up now; I should have your friends here within the next hour or so."

Damarie decided to phone the house and check on J. Candace answered, "Hey son, everything alright?"

"Everything's good here, may I speak to J?"

Candace put down the phone and yelled out for J. J picked up "Hey boo, thanks for my necklace, it's so beautiful." Damarie brushed right over the thank you and asked how she was feeling. "I'm ok." J said.

"Well aright then, I'm going to let you go."

"But wait, you didn't even tell me where you are at." All J heard was a dial tone.

Damarie was pissed at J, and decided that hearing her voice made him even more upset. Esmeralda came into the living room and, "Ah, excuse me do you need anything?"

"Yes, as a matter of a fact I do, I need a drink."

"And what would you like to drink sir?"

"I will take a couple beers and three shots of tequila with salt and limes please."

"Right away sir"

Damarie went out by the pool and started drinking. He began to feel more at ease. Right there, he made a decision to have a good time and leave all of his cares from home behind him.

Ja'Lee and Ryde came in both smiling and laughing. Esmeralda pointed them to the direction of Damarie.

Ryde took a seat while Ja'Lee stood up. "Hey bro, it's beautiful here, let's get changed and head out and do some drinking, which you started without us."

"Sounds like a plan to me. Are you down "Ryde?"

"Yeah, I'm in. I may as well see what the rest of my culture is about while I'm here."

Ryde headed off to her room to shower and change, while Ja'Lee stayed behind to talk to Damarie.

"So what's going on with you, bro?"

"Nothing that I can't handle, it's J. I been catching her in some mad lies lately, missing money, property issues,

Kahladee

and the way she spent that money renovating the property really just blew my mind.

"I feel you bro I think it's time you analyze the situation."

Ja'Lee was relieved that Damarie was starting see J's other side. He felt that a lot of decisions that Raneka made had J's influence.

"Well bro, let's go kick it while we can, cause tomorrow our work begins."

Within an hour everyone was dressed and ready to go, Ryde wore a cantaloupe colored tube dress and gold wedge sandals, Damarie and Ja'Lee both wore linen short sets, Damarie's was taupe colored, and Ja'Lee's was powder blue.

Esmeralda called the transportation service and they were off to experience the night life of the Dominican Republic. They hit up several bars intermixing with the people in the city. Women were all over Damarie and Ja'Lee. They both innocently flirted. Ryde did not have a slow flock of men at her feet either.

When the night ended they were all drunk and rowdy pouring out their sober thoughts. Ryde listened as Damarie and Ja'Lee both complained about their women and the recent drama that surrounded them. Once they got back to the condo they said their drunken goodnights and headed off to bed.

The following day Ryde got up early, and headed out to shop and site see even though she was fluent in Spanish she still felt disconnected. She decided that she would look for her family on one of these trips.

Wednesday came and it was time to head home, it had been a short but delightful trip; It didn't even feel like work to Damarie because ever thing with the drop ran so smoothly.

Chapter 15

Secrets and Lies

Back home Mega and Mija had been inseparable, when he wasn't on the block, he was with her, and when they weren't together, they were calling and texting each other. They were falling for one another fast. J had become so suspicious of Damarie's whereabouts that she managed to talk Raneka into thinking that Ja'Lee and Damarie were both up to no good.

J had come up with a plan to find out just what was going on. J and Raneka planned to go to Damarie's old apartment to talk to one of J's old contacts who could possibly provide them with answers. Although Raneka was skeptical, she followed J's lead.

As soon as Candace left to run her errands, they peeled out. Once at the old apartment, J told Raneka to wait in the car and she would be back in fifteen minutes or less. She headed into the apartment building and went straight to the old unit entering the apartment with key she kept.

Once she was in, she started rummaging through Mega's things but she came up with nothing. Since Mega kept the same home phone number, she decided she would try the password and successfully listened to the voicemail. The first few were from his baby mama begging Mega to be with her. "What a sad and desperate bitch," J thought to as she fast forwarded the message. Another message from some chick named Mija, and finally a message from Damarie… "What's up bro just letting you know we made it and its beautiful here, now if I could just speak a lil' Spanish ha-ha. We will get up when I get back in town later."

J marked the message new and hung up the phone. She decided she would head down to the bedroom and check to see if the combination to the safe was the same, she punched in the numbers 09161977 and whala! It opened. The combination was still Damarie's birthday.

She took roughly 2000 dollars in cash and a brick for old time sake. J headed out to the living looking around to make sure everything was in place. All was clean and clear.

Once she was outside the door she heard giggling, she hurried and locked the door and started walking down the hall. The giggling grew closer as she tried to hurry but she

Kahladee

wasn't fast enough she heard her name and paused. She looked back and it was Mega and some girl. J didn't answer, she just kept going. Mega tried to run her down, but was halted by Mija's voice. "I knew you were too good to be true. Got me coming over to your place and you intrigued at the sight of some girl who can't even answer you?"

Mega tried to calm Mija down but she had been through all the drama before and wasn't having it. She stormed off leaving Mega standing with his arms in the air.

Mega open the door to his apartment and right away he could smell perfume. He took a look around the crib but nothing looked out of place. He sat down trying to figure out what just happened; he asked himself "was that J? Naw it couldn't be, she was not physically capable." I'm losing my mind he thought. He didn't know what to think, so he dialed her phone, no answer. He kept making up excuses for her, she's probably at home looking at the phone thinking why the fuck am I calling her?

Mega gave it no more thought, Mija reentered his mind, I fucked up and I got to make this right. He called Mija, when she answered he began by telling her that he could explain if she gave him the chance. He also told her that there were no other women in his life besides his mother. Mija just listened to him. "Look Boo, I been here before and I don't plan on revisiting my past so just come by my place tonight and we can talk. I need to see your eyes. I am a big believer that eyes don't lie."

"What time should I be there? He politely asked?"

"8pm is fine."

Mega hung up the phone glad she was willing to see him and hear him out. J made it to the car, she was breathing heavy.

"Raneka asked what the fuck happened? Did you find out something out?"

"Yeah, more than I bargained for." she answered. "just let catch my breath and we will talk. I'm in pain."

Raneka started driving back toward the house. It took J a minute to get her thoughts together she knew she couldn't lose control of the situation. She thought long and hard. I just have to go back and put this all back before he misses it. I know he saw me. If Damarie knew he would leave me. I can't afford to be caught up like this.

Raneka looked at J, "Well spit it out." J responded,

"I want to tell you, but I'm afraid of what shit this might do to you."

"Just tell me."

"Ok ok, Ja'Lee is cheating on you. I don't have all the facts yet, but he has been seeing this girl."

"Who is she?"

Kahladee

I don't know Raneka, some girl name Mija. Promise me you will keep this under wraps until I have all the facts, you have to act like nothing's changed, Raneka."

"You have my word. What did you find out about Damarie?"

"Nothing," she answered.

They pulled into the driveway and headed inside the house to get themselves together. It would only be amount of time before the fellas were home.

Damarie and the crew had landed in New Jersey, met up with "Work" to discuss plans for the next few trips.

They sewed up the next few dates and headed home.

Several hours later Mega headed over to Mija's loft to talk to her. He arrived on time and to his surprise, she had cooled down, she invited him in and offered him a drink.

"Listen Mija, I apologize, it's not what you think. I thought I saw my son's mother's friend snooping around my apartment, but I was mistaken."

"Mega its ok, I overreacted, I'm sorry, let's not let something so small come between a good thing."

With that said, Mega and Mija just sat back and chilled the rest of the evening both falling asleep on the couch. Mija woke up by the sound of keys jingling in the door, she rose up, and there was Dameta standing there, she looked like she had seen a ghost.

Mija asked eagerly how her trip was. It was good Mija tapped Mega on the arm he got up yawning and asking what time it was. Before Mija answered he looked over and saw "Ryde." He too was shocked. Mija reintroduced the two; Dameta shook his hand, "nice to meet you." By her response, he knew to keep silent.

Mega got off the sofa, kissed Mija, and headed for the door, "I will let you two catch up. Nice meeting you again Dameta he said sarcastically."

"Yeah, you too" she responded.

Mega left thinking to himself "this is the strangest day I have ever encountered." He headed home to have a drink and pop a couple Ativan to ease his mind. Raneka was trying to keep it together, but was having a hard time since J told her the news. When Ja'Lee picked her up she was silent. He kept asking what was wrong but couldn't get a straight answer.

He figured she was just annoyed with being stuck with J for too long and left her alone.

Damarie tried to come home and relax but couldn't because J had fifty questions, which led straight to an argument. For once this was this is the reaction she wanted. Damarie left extremely pissed and she left soon after. She knew she had at least two hours before he would return.

Kahladee

He rode around for about thirty min before he decided to call "Ryde." When she picked up, he asked if he could swing by and talk to her. She told him that would be fine and to head over. J drove back to Mega's apartment. She had developed a plan that would keep him from telling on her.

She circled the complex to see if there were any lights on and she found that there weren't. She headed up to the apartment and crept inside. It didn't appear that he was home so she headed down the hall to return the money and the brick.

When she got closer to the room, she could see that the door was cracked; she peeped in and saw that he was passed out. She tried to ease her way in but knew she didn't have a chance if he heard the buttons to the safe. She began to panic, she could see the gun on the night stand, and she knew from his past, he would pull the trigger without thought.

J eased the door opened and stood at the foot of the bed, she slowly climbed in rubbing on his legs easing her way up to his dick, she began to give him head, he started to moan out, "Mija, baby damn you crazy girl I love you." Mega was high as hell, from all the drinking and pills he had taken. J slid off his boxers and sat her elf on him and began to ride him. He just kept calling out Mija's name. Mega woke up suddenly, realizing Mija didn't have a key to his apartment. He opened his eyes and it was J. He tried to refocus his eyes thinking he was in a dream. She put her hands around his mouth and told him to listen, as she continued to ride him.

"Look you dumb fuck, it was me you saw earlier, and if you say anything to my man, I will tell him about our brief encounter here tonight. He won't find your words to be true once he figures out you're not loyal; there's missing money, a whole brick missing from the safe, and you fucked his woman raw. Mega came right after that, J got up kissed him on the forehead, put her clothes on and left him lying there in shock.

J headed home to shower and change for bed. Damarie was still out when she got home. It didn't dawn on her until she got home, what she had done, she wasn't on the pill, she really didn't know if Mega was disease free, and last but not least, she had just cheated on her man.

She took a long hot shower and a pain pill to ease her mind and her body. Damarie and Ryde had been sitting in truck the whole time talking about everything when he realized what time it was, he figured he would go home before J started calling.

He got out the truck to walk Ryde to the door of her building. He went in for a hug but ended up kissing her. Ryde stood there in shock, Damarie apologized and walked off. Deep down he wasn't sorry, he really liked what he saw in her, but was in love with J.

He needed to get his shit together, he had taken it too far, and he broke the code. He sped off in a hurry and made it home quick. When he got in the drive way, he texted

Kahladee

Ryde "I'm sorry, it won't happen again let's forget that ever happened."

Ryde texted back "I don't know what you're talking about" with that he smiled, and headed into the house.

J was sitting up in bed when he came in guilt ridden. He apologized to her. For the first time she didn't have much to say. She kissed on him and made love to him. To him there was no need for words when a woman with broken ribs and a broken arm would still try to satisfy him.

It had been three weeks since all the drama had taken place; everyone was trying to get back into the swing of things. The crew was getting ready to make their second drop. Raneka and Ja'Lee were doing fine. She was just keeping a close watch on him, Mega put the money back that J stole and lucky for him she left the brick behind, and best of all he and Mija were on the upswing.

Ryde and Damarie managed to keep their relationship business only, even after their mishap. J had been sick the last few weeks and decided to go into the clinic and get checked out. All of her test came back negative, except one. Her pregnancy test had come back positive. She was excited and phoned to tell Damarie right away. Damarie baby, I know we wanted to wait a year or two but God has planned for us to have a baby now, I'm pregnant.

Damarie sat on the phone in silence. "J are you sure?"

"Yes baby I'm sure that's why I've been so sick. Aren't you happy baby?"

"Yeah I'm happy, I'm just shocked and with the crew right now so I will meet you at home in a half hour and we will celebrate."

"J hung up the phone with tears in her eyes; she was going to be the mother of Damarie Jackson's first born."

She hung up the phone and it dawned on her "oh my God, what if it's not Damarie's?"

Damarie put the phone down and dropped his head. Ja'Lee, "Ryde," and Mega all asked what was wrong. Damarie replied and said "I'm going to be a dad."

No one seemed to know how to react. Mega got a real sick feeling and all kind of crazy thoughts entered his mind, "What if it's mine? What the fuck would I tell Mija? Damarie is my boy; I can't let shit go down like this."

Ryde sat thinking that the man she loved deep down would never be hers. Ja'Lee kept thinking, "I don't want this for my bro, not with that bitch."

Damarie headed home stopping to pick up bottle of Moet for himself, flowers, and sparkling cider for J. He walked in the house to find her crying and whimpering. He went over to her and asked what was wrong? She stated, "I know you don't want this baby. I could tell it in your voice over the phone. We have options. I don't want you to be unhappy with me."

Kahladee

"J, we both knew I wasn't ready yet, but I was preparing myself for the next year or two to be a father. But if you're pregnant now, then we are having this baby, bottom line. I don't know what options you're talking about, but a aborting my seed ain't an option if that's the road you were heading down."

J knew Damarie didn't believe in abortion and wouldn't hear of it, but she also thought about the consequences of the baby belonging to another man. As Damarie sat trying to comfort J, she tuned him out and reflected on her dirty secrets, trying to plot and plan a way out of all this mess she created. Maybe I should abort the baby and just tell him I lost it or I will just have the baby he will think it is his. I can't take any more risks. What if God punishes me and I am never blessed with another baby? J was stuck ... How did I get here? She began to think back.

Chapter 16

Raw and Dirty Reflections

How could she be so stupid she thought, not only did she fuck Mega, but she took a trip to Jersey a few days after the incident to meet up with "Work" to see if he would pillow talk about where Damarie was doing business.

She set him up big time J had the contact number and although they had never met face to face they spoke on the phone a few times. She called him up and sold him a story about one of her female clients that wanted to get into business on her own, "Work" didn't think anything of it and told her to send her up to see him, She told him the clients name was Raneka and when to expect her.

It never crossed "Work's" mind when she told him not to mention it to Damarie. "Work" just assumed that Raneka had problems with Damarie's squad. When J arrived at

Work's place that day, she was in amazement of his home. Although, Damarie had explained that "Work" had money, she was still in awe.

She rang the doorbell; she was let in by a maid and led back to "Work's" office. He stood up and introduced himself, "you must be Raneka" while kissing her hand softly.

"Work" had a thing for women, but a true lust for black women. J took a seat and began to discuss business. She made "Work" comfortable and their conversation went from business to casual in moments. "I got him" she said to herself, he moved closer to her and began to tell her how he admired her beauty,

She tried to keep to the conversation about business, bringing up Damarie every chance she got.

"Yes, he's a good loyal person, that's why I'm shocked you want to leave his squad, especially now that he has only gotten bigger, but with that said, I admire a woman who wants her own start in life. Or is it that you don't care for the new female on his squad?"

"I don't like her at all J spat, and I don't like the direction he's taking things."

"I see"

"Work" moved in on her putting his hand on her lap. He started talking to her about how great of a team they would make and the next thing J knew "Work" was all over her, kissing and caressing her.

They ended up on top of his desk having sex. J laid there momentarily before jumping up. She tried to pull herself together asking "Work" if she could use the restroom. He pointed her into the direction of the bathroom; she scurried past him with her head down once in the bathroom she started opening cabinets and drawer looking for things to clean herself up. Luckily, there were clean towels and toiletries. She pulled her panties off and filled the sink with hot water. She washed her face first and the proceeded to wash up while coming out of the rest of her clothing. She washed vigorously, as if she could wash off the sex she shared with "Work."

"Why did I let this shit happen?" She thought.

She dried off, put her clothing on and headed back out to "Work's" office. "Work" had straightened up while she was in the bathroom. He stared at her as she took a seat.

Worked walked over to her, sat on the arm of the chair; and said "I hope this won't be our only encounter."

"No it won't be because we have business to discuss and I prefer to keep the two separate. Which leads me to discuss money; I need lots of it, that's why I want to go out on my own. I don't need middle men or women for that matter."

"Work" raised his eyebrows, "Well look, right now I'm doing business locally and internationally, and I'll need help as I venture into other areas."

Kahladee

"Where are you doing international business at?"

"The Dominican Republic," he answered, "But I have a full team there, plus you said you didn't want any middle men. So why don't you let me put some things together my sweet and get back to you. Until then, just stay pretty and sexy for me."

"Work" pulled open his desk draw and passed her a gold envelope, "this should help keep you occupied in the meantime."

She extended her hand and accepted the envelope. Then she stood up and kissed him on the cheek. "I must be going now. I will call you soon. Thanks for everything," J walked out feeling extremely nasty deep down inside, she just traded sex for information and money.

As she approached her car, she opened the envelope and there was nothing in it but crisp hundred dollar bills. It had to be about four thousand dollars. "Well, I might as well do some shopping." She got in the car and dialed Damarie's mom. Mrs. Belle picked up

"Hello."

"Hey Mrs. Belle, how are you?"

"I'm fine, is Damarie ok?"

"Yes he is fine."

She chuckled, "Oh ok. I'm just not used to hearing from you. Are you ok?"

"Yes, I'm fine too. But listen, I'm in the area and I want to take you out are you busy?"

"No I'm not. Come on by sweetie."

When J pulled into the parking lot Mrs. Belle was sitting on the stairs talking on the phone, as J approached Mrs. Belle she could tell she was talking to Damarie by the expressions on her face.

"Yeah Damarie, here she is standing right next to me you want to talk to her?" She passed J the phone.

"Hey baby, what's up?"

"Why didn't you tell me you were driving to Jersey? I've been calling your phone for two hours and your phone kept going straight to voicemail."

"Oh Baby, I'm sorry. I didn't tell you cause I didn't want you to slip and tell mama Belle I was coming up. I wanted to surprise her, take her out to eat, and to do a little shopping. My phone was in the car on the charger, it was completely dead."

"Yeah ok J, but next time please be considerate, I was worried about you."

J told Damarie bye and focused her attention on Mama Belle. "Well, Mama Belle let's hit the streets. We can go anywhere you like, J stated smiling." Mrs. Belle locked up the house and just like that, J and her were off to have some much needed bonding time.

"J!, are you listening to me?" Damarie yelled snap out of it . J opened her eyes "yes baby, I'm sorry, I completely zoned out for a minute. She had been reflecting on the stupid choices she made. "I've got to shake this off and pull myself together" she thought. She cleared her throat, and sat up straight "your right Damarie we are going to have this baby and be the best parents a child could ever have ."

Chapter 17

Drop Two

It was fall, and had only been three months since the news of J's pregnancy. However, by the way she carried herself and begin to act; you would have thought she was due any day. She used her morning sickness to her advantage and quit working, altogether. J went from being needy to handicap within weeks after her pregnancy announcement. She hired a maid, paid her mom to come by and cook meals, and even went as far as having the dry cleaning service come by the house to pick up the dry cleaning. In fact, the only things she managed to get done was her hair, nails, and shopping.

Damarie had been laying low and had not had any contact with anyone except Ja'Lee since the news. A part of him was happy, but the other part of him was fuming because deep down he felt J had gotten pregnant on purpose. On top of that, he could tell what he was in for because even though he told her all the extra spending needed to cease, she just kept spending. Rather than argue, he threw himself even heavier in the game.

He called everyone up, starting with "Ryde;" she answered the phone without looking at the number "Hello."

"Hey, how you doing" he asked?"

"I'm fine, who is this?"

"It's me, Damarie."

"Oh, I didn't catch your voice, what's up?"

"I'm just calling you to let you know it's time to make that move."

"Ok," she replied, "but how soon?"

"Thursday night," he answered sharply, "but we need to hook up before then so I can let you know how things need to go down. Can you meet up with me and the fellas in about an hour?"

"Yeah that should be fine, whereabouts?"

"Meet us at Phatties."

Damarie put the phone down and dialed Mega and Ja'Lee next.

Ryde hung up the phone and begin pacing, she was nervous about seeing Damarie. She quickly showered, rubbed on some Shea butter body cream, and sprayed on a dash of her favorite perfume, Issey Miyake. She finally got dressed wearing a pair of dark wash denim jeans, cognac color riding boots, and a cream long sleeve V-neck top. Dameta tried not to overdo it so she let her hair air dry and only applied lip gloss.

By the time Dameta made it to Phatties, the guys had already ordered drinks; Damarie stood up, and greeted her and pulled out her chair for her. As she got comfortable, Damarie brought her up to speed letting her know that this time it would be her to smuggle the cash this time, and that he wouldn't be accompanying her and Ja'Lee. He would stay back with Mega and handle things on the turf.

"Your flight leaves at six pm on Thursday night so you to will have to leave no later than one in the afternoon to make it to Jersey on time."

"As far as us Mega, we got to hit these streets harder than we have been. We got to get rid of these birds. We will have another shipment in three weeks and we haven't even moved all of our last batch. We can't have all that product out here, too big of a risk, you feel me?"

Mega spoke up, "Yeah I feel you. Let's whip this batter and get this cake. But in order to move this shit any

Kahladee

faster, we are going to have to take on some new turf or muscle somebody off theirs…"

"I don't have a problem doing either one. Just let me know which direction you want take it and consider it done."

Ja'Lee cut in, "He is right Damarie, we are going to have to cover new ground or take somebody else's. Otherwise, we are going to have both shipments for the next six months. And the deal was, we do three drops and we're done as far as that international shit goes."

Damarie spoke up, "Yeah I know guys, that's why I'm staying back to map things out with Mega, cause I feel like we going to be taking over turf, instead of covering new turf. The reality is we're taking on a major risk, no matter what we choose. If cover new area, we risk the fucking cops and if we move in on somebody else's turf, we risk a street war which we all know I'm not a fan of. By the time you and Ryde return on Sunday, we will have done one or the other, that's for sure."

"So Mega, with that being said we will hook up Thursday early and get this product off our hands."

Damarie passed Ja'Lee the tickets, paid the tab, and headed out. Ja'Lee and everyone one else followed suit. Once outside everyone headed their own direction. Mega and Ryde happened to be heading the same way.

Ryde came out and asked Mega, "What are your intentions with my Mija?" He replied, "Not that it's any of your business, but she's my girl and I care about her a lot."

Ryde looked him dead in the eyes before taking another jab at him and then said, "If you hurt my friend, I will take you down myself Mega... I know your type I seen it too many times before."

She could see why Mija was so attracted to him. Underneath that 'don't fuck with me' appearance, he owned beautiful eyes, and a nice charming smile. "Oh really you know my type huh?"

"And just what is my type?"

"You don't want me to answer that," she replied.

"Well I tell you what "Ryde," since we on the subject of hurting others, what would Mija think of you if she knew what kind of position you were holding down? And let's not get on the fact that you got a thing for Damarie knowing he has a woman."

"Ryde's" eyes grew bigger and she was suddenly speechless. "Yeah, I see the way you look at him but I'm not here to judge."

"Look Mega, I just don't want to see her hurt, that's all. This is about my friend; I have no problem with you."

"Ok then "Ryde," let's agree to get along and be friends. I'm on your team, I don't care for that Bitch J, and frankly I would not care if you fucked him in the middle of the street to keep it real. Well, now that we got all this out the way

---

"Ryde," I gotta get going. I'm taking Mija out tonight so I will get at you later."

Deep down, Mega knew Ryde was right about him. He had been the 'love em and leave em' type, but the difference was Mega had feelings for Mija. She touched him mentally and emotionally the way no other women had ever been able to, not even his baby's mother. It was like she had the keys to all the secret doors of his heart and mind. He found himself changing for her. He was never known to wine and dine his women, but now, he found himself out at least three or four times a week with Mija. They went to the movies, fine restaurants, and he even took her shopping.

By the time Ryde made it home it was already 7:30pm. Ryde noticed a black duffle bag sitting on the edge of the couch as she walked down the hall toward her bedroom. She stopped and knocked on Mija's door. Mija opened the door, "Oh hey girl, what's up?"

"Not much, how bout with you?"

"I'm getting ready to go out with my baby," she said smiling.

"Oh he's your baby now?" Dameta asked laughing.

"Yeah well, what can say? I'm digging everything about him. The way he carries himself, his swag, I don't know, just everything. I feel safe with him, you know, and I haven't felt this safe with a guy in a long time, and the crazy part is we haven't even had sex yet. We decided to take things slow, not to rush into anything and as bad as I have wanted to sex him. I haven't pushed the issue because I want him to respect me. Well you know what they say Dameta, there's someone for everybody and I think he is the one for me."

"Mija, I am happy for you and I'm glad you found

that special someone to hold on to. I just want you to be careful because I don't want to see you hurt. Which leads me to the duffle bag on the couch, should I expect you back tonight?"

"As a matter of a fact you can't because I'm staying at his place tonight. It just might just be his lucky night."

Once Mija left for her date with Mega, Dameta decided to clean up around the house and pack up her bags. Once she finished, she figured she better call and pay her bills over the phone. She knew Mija would forget and she would come home to no electricity, cable, and more importantly, no water. She grabbed her Blackberry out of her coat pocket and saw that she had four missed calls and two text messages. Damn, I didn't even hear my phone. She scrolled through the missed call list and noticed two out of the four calls were from Damarie. She called him back,

"Hello."

"Hey Ryde how are you?"

"I'm cool, she answered. What can I do for you?"
"Well, I was calling to check up on you. I know I'm not
going to be going out of town with you but I want you to
know personally you are in good hands with Ja'Lee and if
there is anything you're in doubt about you can tell me."

 Ryde spoke up softly "You know everything is chill on my
end, you have nothing to worry about. I'm sure Ja'Lee and
I will be just fine."

"Alright then Ma, I will be in touch, call me if you need
me."

Ja'Lee woke up early and asked Raneka to call in to work
so he could spend time with her before he left. He felt like
she had been so distant lately and he wanted to clear the
air before he left town. She called in like he asked her to,
but with hesitation. She had a major attitude with Ja'Lee
and she could no longer contain it.

 "Raneka" He yelled her name from the kitchen.

She didn't answer, so he walked back to the bedroom.

"Raneka, I know you hear me"

"Yeah, I do what?"

"What? I'm talking to you, that's what."

"Well, maybe I don't want to talk to you."

"Well, why the fuck you call then Raneka?"

"To make a nigga miserable he asked? You know what you miserable on your own; she spat back it must be hard being stuck up in Damarie's ass all the time."

"Where the hell is this coming from Raneka?"

You been running around with your head up your ass for two months, we aren't touching, fucking, or nothing around here."

"Hell no, we ain't fucking because you got another bitch for the job."

Ja'Lee looked at Raneka with a surprised look on his face.

"Yeah mutha fucka, I know all about you and that weak bitch you fucking."

"What! I ain't fucking anybody, not even you, I don't know where the hell you bought that bullshit, but you need to take it back and get a full refund."

Raneka got out of bed, walked over to the night stand where Ja'Lee always kept his wallet, cell phone, and other belongings.

"What the fuck are you doing?" He asked.

Let's call this bitch you trying to go out of town with, you talking about Damarie's ain't going. Since when, his ass don't leave with you?"

"Look Raneka, he needs to stay with J and do other shit this time. Ain't nobody trying to bring no bitch out of town to fuck, so put my stuff down and quit tripping!" Raneka started going through his phone and he walked over to her reaching his hand out. "Give me my phone baby please."

"Hell no, fuck this phone and you too for that matter."

The next Ja'Lee knew, he had slapped Raneka. She started crying, spazzing out, and throwing shit out of his drawer. She located his passport and other important papers and ripped them to shreds. Ja'Lee grew even madder, he snatched her up, looking her in eye, "Bitch, give me my phone. I'm leaving and when I get back, make sure you and your shits gone. I don't want a trace of you in my sight, you insecure crazy bitch."

Ja'Lee threw on a jogging suit, grabbed his keys, his spare cell phone off the charger, and dipped out. He sat in his new Audi and dialed Damarie and before Damarie could even say hello, he began to ramble off about how Raneka flipped out on him and ripped up his passport. "Man bro, the bitch went nuts, accusing me of cheating, being in your ass all types of shit. Before I knew it, I slapped her and snatched her lil' ass up. I regret hitting her, but I put her ass out anyway. Fuck that crazy ass shit.

Damarie finally got to speak "Man bro, I don't know what to say about this shit, it's crazy. Are you cheating on her?"

"Hell no bro, you know I would tell you."

"Right man, I know. What you need me to do?"

"Well I obviously can't go on this run with no passport so we got to get you a plane ticket; I'm going to have to stay here with Mega. I need to lay low any how ain't no telling what kind of revenge Raneka got in store for me."

"Man Ja'Lee give her a little time, apologize for your wrong in it and y'all get that shit together, feel me?"

"Yeah, I feel you, but it's best she get out like I told her to. I can't deal with that shit right now."

"Alright bro, get that shit at home together, plan on hooking up with Mega once you got your home situation under wraps, so we can be right in the streets. I will get a ticket and head out with Ryde this evening, when I get back in town, we will hook up."

Damarie called Mega, told him there was a change in plans, and Ja'Lee would fill him in later. He dialed "Work" next to let him know things were on schedule but to have his people expect him at the condo instead and the cash drop would still be made by "Ryde." Now the hard part was telling J he had to leave town. She was asleep when he made it back to the bedroom. He started going through the closet putting outfits together. J was awakened by the sounds of him moving around the room. She rolled over and asked him what he was doing.

"I'm packing" he stated.

"For what?" she asked.

'I got to go out of town this evening baby, I know it's last minute, but Ja'Lee can't do it now."

Kahladee

"Why can't he go?"

"Because baby, he got some things going on with Raneka."

"What he got going with her? She's not the one pregnant."

Look Ma, I got to go and that's that, I'm sure she will be calling you later today cause they ain't doing well. J, you act like pregnancy is a handicap or some shit, you wanted a baby and being pregnant is major part of having a baby, so don't get to complaining now. Somebody got to bring paper in here to pay for all this shit we have. You obviously can't because you quit your job and you stopped hustling so deal with it."

J rolled back over pulling the covers over her head muttering under her breath "Whatever, Damarie."

By the time I made home from the gym and running last minute errands, it was already 3pm, I walked in the house and Mija was sitting on the couch watching TV. I walked over to her, snatched the remote out of her hands, and turned off the TV. She looked up at me smiling. Before she could open her mouth, I started going in her." Damn bitch, you home two days later." I said laughing. "I started to put an APB out on your hoe ass. That was the longest date I ever seen you go on. It must have been more than Mega's lucky night." Mija busted out laughing.

"Hell to the naw, it wasn't just his lucky night; it was his lucky night, morning, afternoon, evening, and next day.

We got it on, bitch, he brought his A game. I'm so discombobulated; all I can do is sit here and look dumb as hell. He got me walking funny, and my 'girl' is all swollen, I had to soak in the tub for like an hour."

"Well, that's what you get ha-ha. You said you wanted to sex him, but it seems like you're the one who got sexed, punk. But on a lighter note I am glad you're home, I forgot to tell you I was leaving town again, I paid all the bills, and as you can see, I cleaned up the house, I left the laundry for you but now if you too sore to do it, I can do when I get back ha-ha. Mija, I'm going to take a shower and a nap, can you wake me up by five please? I'm leaving at six."

"Yeah I can do that, where are you going by the way and with who?"

I paused before answering. "Actually, I'm going to the Islands for this job I'm considering, I will be back on Sunday." I hated lying to Mija, but I knew I couldn't tell her the truth right now. I would eventually though; we didn't keep secrets from each other that was a pact we had since grade school.

Mija woke me up at five just like I asked her to, I got up and got dressed, and placed my Michael Kors luggage set by the doorway, so I could be ready when Ja'Lee pulled up. I sat on the chair by the window watching out for him. Mija was stretched out on the couch, still going on about how sore she was. All I could do was laugh at her because she swore up and down that she was 'Miss Beasty Sheets.' I glanced out the window and looked

Kahladee

down at my watch; it was six on the dot. It was dark out but I saw head lights, so I headed down. Once outside, I saw it was Damarie's truck but I didn't think much of it and proceeded to walk down the sidewalk toward the truck. I heard a door open and shut, it was Damarie. I gave him a surprised look, he looked at me and said "It's a long story, but as you can see, there has been a change of plans, it's me and you on this run. He grabbed my backs and put them in the truck. I got in, put on my seat belt, and we were off.

We didn't talk much on the way to Jersey but once we were at the airport we started to go over the routing. I had the money in my carry-on bag. I secured it tight just like Damarie told me to. Damarie went to another line to be checked in, he was on the same flight, but would be seated in a different section than me. I checked in and headed to the security line, being careful not to seem nervous or on edge. As I got closer, I started taking off my shoes so I could be ready. I placed my bag with the money in it on the conveyor belt and everything else in the scanning bins. A security guard started waving his wand across my body; it started beeping around my waist. "Damn, what the fuck?" I thought. I kept looking to see if my bag made it through, I couldn't tell. The guard asked me if I had any metal on and I couldn't think of anything, but then I remembered that I wore a dumb ass Gucci belt. I replied "oh yeah, my belt." I took it off and put it on the bin. The guard waved the wand across my body again, it didn't beep this time, I walked through to the gate and my carry-on bag was there. "I made it, whew"

Kahladee

Chapter 18

Feels Right

It was the same routine as last when we touched down. "Paper" picked us up on schedule, dropped us off at the condo, Esmeralda greeted us with a smile, and asked if we needed anything. Even though she had only met us once, you could tell she was happy to see us. Damarie hugged her, told her he was just fine, and I did the same, but the truth was I was ready to dive into some serious alcohol. I was still in shock that I was going to be in this condo with Damarie for the whole weekend and I was nervous as hell. Trying to act chill, I headed for the bar myself; I poured myself a shot of Patrón and took it straight to the head, making sure to keep a straight face. Damarie looked at me as I poured another shot, "Damn 'Ryde,' you ok?" he asked. I answered swiftly "Yeah I'm cool, just trying to relax a little before tomorrow. I know the hard part is over so I figure, I may as well unwind and have a good time."

"I have a better idea 'Ryde,' why don't we get changed and hit the scene? We don't make the official drop until tomorrow evening, anyhow."

"It sounds like a plan to me" I answered.

"Ok well, I'll head back to my room to take a shower, change, and make a couple of calls and then we can bounce." I watched Damarie as he strutted down the hall, I know he can feel me watching him, I thought. Just before he turned to enter the room, I turned my head to talk to Esmeralda .

"Esmeralda, it appears we are going to head out for a couple cocktails, so if you prefer to turn in, it's cool with me."

Esmeralda answered me smiling, "If I were your age, I would have more than cocktails with him."

In shock, all I could do was start laughing. She winked and passed me a card with her number on it, "Call me if you need anything sweetie. Also call me when you two wake up in the morning, I will make you both a nice breakfast."

"Sure thing, Esmeralda, thank you so much for your hospitality." Once Esmeralda left, I scurried to my room to change and freshen up. I kept on the same jeans, changed shirts, bumped my bob out a little, and lastly, I

Kahladee

freshened my makeup. As I headed back out to the bar, I could hear Damarie's phone conversation; it appeared to be his girl.

"Look baby, I know this was last minute. I already explained it to you, the plan is to be back on Sunday, but if I can, I will be back sooner. If you need anything, call your mom. And by the way, did you hear from Raneka yet?"

J answered "Yes, as a matter of fact I did, and I'm on her side. He had no business putting his hands on her. He's the one cheating. I told her she could stay with us until she finds a new place."

"You did what?" Damarie spat back.

"I told her she could stay here until she found a place."

"No! Don't get into their shit, what the fuck that look like J, he's my boy."

"Yeah and that's my girl and I'm going to be here for her."

"Well J, there is other ways you could be there without getting directly in between the fire. Damn, you kill me sometimes. Listen I have to go J, we will talk about this when I get home, love you, bye." Damarie headed out of the room shutting the door behind him. I was seated on the eggshell colored Natuzzi leather sectional with my legs crossed. As he grew closer, I smelled Creed cologne.

165

I could point out that scent anywhere; one of the partners back at the firm always wore it. Damarie was wearing a burnt orange colored sweater, gold colored Levis, brown leather shoes that I had never even seen before so I couldn't put a name to them, and a pair of wood framed Cartier eye glasses with gold accents. He walked to the bar, poured himself a glass of Cognac, and sat himself next to me.

"So lil' lady, we better call for a ride so we can get a lil' of this night life." Damarie picked up the house phone and dialed "Paper," the phone rang and rang, but "Paper" didn't pick up.

Damarie looked at me and shrugged his shoulders. "I guess he will call us back when he sees the missed call."

"Yeah I guess so," I replied. Before we knew it, an hour had passed with no return call from "Paper." It was chill though, we found ourselves entrenched in a deep conversation or more like a therapy session. I was the counselor. Damarie told me all about the problems, he and J had within the last six months. He told me of all the plans he had for himself. I shared mine as well; we shared a natural emotional connection.

We gave up on Paper two to three drinks into our conversation we were laughing and cracking jokes. I was feeling good and tipsy so I decided to call it a night. As I stood to leave, Damarie grabbed my hand pulling me back down on the sofa. I landed right in his lap. He flipped me over on the couch landing on top of me kissing and caressing me. He lifted me off the couch and carried me

Kahladee

to his room laying me on the bed. We undressed each other and the kissing continued. I opened my legs and he entered me gently, but aggressive. Damarie's hands were like magic, I could cum just from his touch alone. It was the first time in my life as a lawyer that I didn't object the plaintiff, it was a case I was more than willing to lose.

I woke up the next morning in Damarie's arms. I looked around for a clock but I didn't see one. I didn't see my clothes either. I gently slid out of his arms pulling the sheet with me trying to be careful not wake him. I tip toed toward the door but just as I cracked the open, Damarie awoke.

"Hey mama, where are you sneaking off to?"

I answered "Oh, I was just going to take a shower."

"Let me dirty you up a lil' more before you hit the water."

I turned around crawled back in bed obviously not turning down his request. We woke up about four hours later to the sound of the phone ringing; Damarie reached over me and answered it.

"Hello"

It was "Work."

"Hey, what's up man?"

"Not much, just calling to check in on you two."

"Oh yeah, everything is chill on this end, just been lounging around all day."

"Well that's good; Esmeralda told me she hadn't heard a peep out of either one of you today."

"Yeah, I decided to sleep in and I bet Ryde did too, but I'm getting up now so we can make that drop and head back home tomorrow.

"Work" spoke up "Well just let me know if you need anything."

"Alright talk to you tomorrow, 'Work'." Damarie said and hung up the phone. Shortly after, he kissed me on the cheek and said "Well 'Ryde' it's time to get down to business."

I rolled over once again taking the sheet with me and headed out the door. As walked out, I bumped right into Esmeralda. I screamed and she screamed too, but we both started laughing. I proceeded to my room feeling partly embarrassed that she caught me leaving his room. I showered, dressed, and headed out to the kitchen. Damarie had already made it out and he was sitting at the kitchen table eating brunch. Esmeralda had prepared quite the spread, French toast, steak, bacon, omelets, fried potatoes, and fresh squeezed orange juice. We ate and chilled out until it was time to make the drop.

Kahladee

Chapter 19

The Block gets Hot

Even though Damarie and Ryde had only been gone for two days, Mega had gotten right down to business. He made a call to his old boy Dollar, to find who out who was fucking their crew out of money and underserving their customers. It wasn't too big of a shocker for Mega to find out it was his old partner in crime Chilla., Mega and Chilla went way back they banged the same set and were once inseparable; you usually didn't see one without the other, it wasn't until Mega did his nickel piece in the state penitentiary that Mega discovered that his longtime friend was anything but his friend. Chilla envied Mega and everything that Mega had established. Even though when Mega ate, Chilla got full, but that wasn't enough for Chilla so when Mega got locked up he went after everything

Mega had, his women, his cars, his look, and most importantly, his place on the concrete. Mega decided it was time to dig in on some much needed revenge and make some money at the same time. Later on that day, Mega met up with Ja'Lee at Chauncey's for lunch to discuss his discovery. Mega could see Ja'Lee wasn't his normal self, so he decided to make the conversation quick. Ja'Lee had already ordered drinks, Mega quick told him who's turf they would move in on with Ja'Lee's permission. Mega wanted to do it as early as tonight. Ja'Lee's answer to Mega was "as long as you can hold down anything you start, I'm in on it." Mega spoke up, "alright bro, I got this. I'm on it; you just kick back and take care of yourself because I can see you're bothered by something. Mega put a fifty dollar bill on the table, put on his coat and headed out. On his way out he passed J and Raneka not thinking anything of it, he spoke and kept going. Both of them waved to him, but once he went past J asked sarcastically, "Raneka, who you think he was here with?" Raneka shrugged her shoulders "How am I supposed to know?"

"Well get up and go see if Ja'Lee is here."

Raneka stood up and begin to walk toward the back of the restaurant looking around to see if she could spot him. She didn't see him so she headed for the ladies room instead, just as she was about to enter the restroom Ja'Lee was walking out of the men's room. She rolled her eyes at him "I know you see me."

Ja'Lee spat back "Yeah, I do, now if you would excuse me." He started walking away from her. Raneka stood

Kahladee

there not knowing what to do so she followed him, grabbing and tugging on him. He turned around to her and asked "Ain't you had enough of trying to fight me?" And now to top it off, you in Chauncey's showing yo ass in front of all these people."

"I just want to talk to you Lee…"

"Well, you had the chance to do that and you didn't want to hear what I had to say; you was too busy acting all insecure and needy. I told you I wasn't cheating on you but my word obviously ain't what you need or believe in so go on with all yo bullshit." Raneka got back in his face and in an attempt to remove some of her embarrassment said "I know all about you and that bitch you fucking and your plans to go out of town, the whole nine." Before he knew it, Ja'Lee blurted out "Raneka, you don't know a damn thing cause that girl you talking about is one of my business partners, not that it's your business. I'm not in yo shit like that." By now they had drawn a crowd and the manager came over and asked them to both leave. Ja'Llee headed to his table grabbing his leather off the chair, but Raneka was fast on his heels. In a last attempt to regain his attention, she called him an "arrogant bitch" and before he knew it, he hauled off and smacked her. She hit the floor crying and screaming "someone call the police." He ran over to her trying to apologize and help her but people were now swarming all over the restaurant, some leaving, some helping Raneka, and others gawking at him. J ruffled through the crowd getting in Ja'Lee's face, "You took this way too far, Lee how you could do this?" Ja' Lee brushed passed her so he could make his exit before the cops arrived. He knew he had to get home. He never kept dope in his apartment but he knew he had guns and other things that could jeopardize his freedom. Once he got to the car he called Mega, told him to meet him at his crib fast and he would explain things later. They pulled up at the same time hurrying into the building. "Man Bro, she got the police on my ass, I snapped on her in Chauncey's and she's calling the cops, take the guns and anything else that's a threat."

"Ok bro, I got you, but what the hell you gonna do?"

"Ain't nothing I can do, but lay low until they pick my ass up. Which means you got to take that block on your own. I'm too hot to move around and ain't no telling what she gonna tell the police. So I'm gonna hit up Damarie to see if he can get back early cause I slipped up and told Raneka that we have a female partner and I know she gonna tell J and that's going to start a whole bunch of other problems we don't need. You feel me?"

"Yeah, I feel you bro. I'm gonna get ghost before them boys show up."

Once Mega was gone Ja'Lee called Damarie, told him he was going in for a domestic with Raneka and he should probably head back home early, to try to get a handle on things before they got in worse.

Back at Chauncey's, the manager on duty escorted J and Raneka to the back office; He hoped removing them

Kahladee

would calm down the rest of the customers. Moments later two officers arrived, a male and a female, they took a few statements from customers and then spoke to Raneka. They took a few pictures of her, her statement, and proceeded to tell her how to file a restraining order. Just like that Ja'Lee became a wanted man and the police wasted no time picking him up. J, tried to fix Raneka up a little bit before heading out of Chauncey's. Her face was still red and stinging, but most of all, she was embarrassed. They scurried out to the car as fast as they could but still managed to gain a few stares. J had been trying for about an hour to reach Damarie, but he didn't answer her calls. She didn't want to say it out loud but deep down she had a feeling that she was the one being cheated on. She couldn't wait to start pecking away at the puzzle. She knew they had a female partner but she had no idea that the bitch was out of town with her man. She was mad as hell. Damn, she thought if I hadn't told Raneka Ja'Lee was cheating, Damarie would be home, and her man would be out of town with the bitch, not mine. She took her mind off the situation and focused on Raneka "Damn Neka, you took this shit too far. I told you not tell him you suspected anything and you had to go losing your cool." Raneka sat sobbing. She could barely utter a word, her voice crackling and her eyes full of tears, she turned and asked J "What if the shoe was on the other foot, how would've you handle it? Could you turn over and fuck, suck, kiss, and be there for your man if he was cheating with some bitch?" J didn't answer her, she just sighed. "Yeah, just like I thought, you couldn't"

Late that night, Mega picked up Dollar and headed over to Chilla's part of town. He had Dollar park two blocks over and kept his Navigator running. He got out of the truck and walked the two blocks he had studied earlier that that evening, just to see the kind of activity was going on. It didn't surprise him that Chilla organized his blocks the way he'd taught him. Chilla was such a swagger jacker; you could predict his every move. He crossed the street and stood on the opposite end of the block. He pulled the hood up from his black leather Pelle Pelle jacket. The three men at the other end hadn't noticed him yet. He dialed his boy Nez on his cell. Nez picked up "yeah?"

"Hit the block, homie"

"Alright, I'm on my way."

Mega had his boy Nez posted on the other block in an old black Cutlass Supreme. Nez hit the block rolling past the men on the corner and pulled up to Mega. Mega walked up to the car asking Nez what he needed loudly so the men could hear. He pretended to serve Nez, told him to park, and wait on the other end of the corner until shit popped off. Mega knew an unknown man serving on their block would gain their attention. Just as he thought, the three men approached him. One was short, fat, and dark skinned, the other two, were tall, light, and lanky, and looked just alike. One of the tall men spoke up in a raspy,

---

yet rather strong tone, "Uhh bra this block is taken, you need to move around...."

Mega just stood there like he didn't hear him..."Ahh bra, move the fuck around, this our shit." Mega looked him in the eye and told him "Bitch this block mine now, so y'all move around or get moved around." The short fat dude walked up and pushed Mega. Mega pushed him back and he landed on his ass, Mega then turned to him and pointed a Glock 9 at him and told him, "Bitch touch me, or say anything and I will wet yo fat ass up." The other two men both backed up and it was now apparent that they were twins. "Thing one and thing two, move to the front now and get Chilla on the phone." They both looked at him in shock. "You heard me, get the mutha fucka on the phone." One of the twins pulled out his phone and dialed Chilla. Chilla answered "This better be business." Mega snatched the phone never taking his eyes off the men. He spoke in the phone "Chilla this Mega, and these scared ass pussy's you got on your team let me serve on yo block, so now it's mine. In fact, I'm taking 5 of your blocks and you can't do shit about it. Chilla yelled in the phone "Bitch you ain't taking shit, you weak muthafucker."

"Chilla, please don't disrespect me, you know how this shit work. I served and it's mine. You jacked my set up, but you don't want to play by the rules?"

"Naw, I ain't playing by your rules. I play by mine. The game has changed Mega and ain't no place for you in it."

"Oh really? Mega asked.

"Yeah really, alright Chilla have it your way," and he hung up the phone. Mega signaled for Nez, Nez pulled down the street in the beater car. He told the twins to get in the back of the car. He then shot out the street light with the Glock turned to the fat guy and said "You never push a nigga without being ready to fight or die. I hope you ready to die." The fat guy was now shaking. Mega looked him in the eye and shot him in the neck killing him instantly. He got in the car sitting in the back with the twins instructing them to direct him and Nez to the other areas of Chilla's turf. Each block they hit, Mega shot folks up, by the time they were done; he had covered 6 blocks. When he was done, he had the twins call Chilla. Chilla picked up the phone. Mega simply said "I changed my mind, I took 6 of your blocks and now I got your twins working for me. I will get at you later cause you going to be busy regrouping and attending funerals."

Kahladee

Chapter 20

Thinking of a Master Plan

Damarie had seen J's calls, but given the incident with Ja'Lee and Raneka he didn't want to answer his phone until he was on his way home. Ja'Lee told him that he got so mad that he slipped up and blurted out that they had a female partner. Damarie was pissed at Ja'Lee for being so stupid, but he knew it wasn't the time to address the issue. Ja'Lee had given Raneka too much control over the situation. She caused him not to make the drop, to be on his way to jail, and gave the cops a reason to look into his character, and now caused Ryde to be out of town on business unexpectedly. Damarie phoned "Work" and told him there was going to be a change of plans and that Ryde would make the drop on her own because he had to leave. "Work" felt a little uneasy about Ryde doing the drop on her own but he had to deal with it. "Work" called one of his assistants to help Damarie get situated so he could leave and take care of whatever he needed to. Ryde knew Damarie was miserable so she didn't press him instead she helped him pack, and told him "I will do whatever you need me to do."

"Ryde baby, I'm sorry to make you do all this by yourself, but I will make it up to you, I promise. I will pick you up in Jersey when your flight lands."

Damarie headed home, Ryde made the drop, and came back and packed up. She called home to check on Mija. When she called, her call went straight to Mija's voicemail. She called back 30 minutes later and Mija picked right up.

"Hello" Mija answered like she was sleep.

"Bitch, don't try to play like you sleep cause your man at the crib."

Mija immediately busted up laughing.

"Girl, he just left so shut up…well, any way what you want?"

"I just wanted to call and let you know that I will be home late tomorrow night and there are some things that I have to talk to you about. I haven't been straight forward with you about a few things, but I don't want you to worry because I'm fine."

"Ok Dameta, I will see you when you get home so we can catch up."

"Sounds like a plan" Dameta responded.

Damarie called J once he was back at the airport and had already checked his luggage for the flight home.

"Damarie, I've been calling you all fucking day. Why the hell, haven't you returned my call?"

"I'm returning it now, ain't I? What is it? What's so important J?"

"Well for starter's Ja'Lee done went crazy and slapped Raneka and to top it off, you out of town with some bitch?"

"First of all, I don't got nothing to do with Ja'Lee and Raneka. Second, it ain't none of your business who I'm doing business with. All you need to do is mind yours and let me handle mines."

"You are my business Damarie, and all I wanna know is how come you couldn't tell me you had a female working with you...Why are you acting so secretive, Damarie? Are you fucking her?"

"Hell no, I ain't fucking her and that's exactly why I didn't tell you cause I don't want to hear that kid of shit. I gotta go J; I will be home in the morning bye."

J knew exactly what she was doing. She wanted to know when he would be back so she could find out more about this girl they had working with them. She knew exactly where to go to find out. She only had a little time on her hands before Damarie was home. She had to get rid of Raneka and head to Jersey to see "Work". She phoned "Pamper Me Spa" to order a deluxe 8 hour package for Raneka. This would give her enough time to see "Work" and get back home.

"Uhh Raneka..."

"Yeah J?"

"I have a surprise for you, you really been going through a lot, so get cleaned up and let's go now missy."

Raneka didn't ask any questions, she just changed and they headed right out. An hour later, J pulled into the spa, they walked in and J gave the receptionist her credit card and told her to give her friend the works. J also said "If I'm not back to pick her up within 8 hours, order a cab on my card for her please."

Raneka asked "J, aren't you going to get a treatment?"

"No Raneka, this is for you. I'm going to go home, clean the house, and rest. So I will see you later ok."

J got in the car and headed to see "Work" she really dreaded the drive but she had a mission. It took her 4 hours instead of the usual 3 because she had to pull over at least four times to pee; the baby was really starting to where on her bladder. She got out of the car pulling and tugging on her blouse even though J was five months pregnant you could only tell when she wore form fitting tops. She went up to the door and the maid answered, telling her that "Work" was in a meeting and could not be disturbed. J told him to tell him Raneka was here and demanded to see him now, it was serious business. The maid radioed "Work" and told him to come to the front and that it was urgent.

"Invite her in and send her back." He told the maid.

J smirked at the maid and brushed passed her and said "I can find my own way thank you." She headed down the hall. She remembered the way like it was yesterday. As she turned toward his office, he was seeing a young black woman out of his office. She headed in and took a seat on the couch. "Work" slammed the door seemingly upset by her showing up unannounced. He turned to her and asks "What are you doing here Raneka?"

"Well, I have some news for you of course signaling him to sit next to her. But first I have to tell you something that could potentially ruin our friendship and to be honest I don't give a fuck if it does."

"Raneka, what is it?"

"Well, let me get to the point. My name is not Raneka, it's J, and I'm Damarie's fiancé…"

"Work" looked at her in shock.

"And if you don't tell me what I want to know and do what I say, I'm going to tell him you tricked me by calling me over here a few months ago and you raped me. He is one of your key payers and I'm sure you don't want to lose him."

"Look you little manipulative bitch, I'm not telling you shit or doing shit for you. In fact I'm going to call him and tell him what a lil' skank ass hoe he has on his hands."

J reached for "Works" hand rubbing it softly telling him "I knew that you would try to under estimate my brain. I'm also five months pregnant with your baby and if you don't want your wife to get an invitation to my baby shower then I suggest you do as I say. I want to know where he is right now and who he is with."

"Work" began to sing to J, like Frankie Lymon, He is with Dameta, but they call her "Ryde." She's a lawyer, real smart, and kind of stuck up. They've been handling business in the Dominican Republic. They fly out of Jersey and there is only one more cash drop to make and then we are done. What does she look like J asked? "Work" went over to his desk drawer and pulled out a picture of Ryde he still had from having her ID made. J looked at the picture trying to see if she could place the face, but she couldn't. She asked more questions "do you know where she's from, where does she live, is she single, does she have kids?" "Work" couldn't answer J, he didn't have the answers. J was agitated as all hell, at this point. She jumped down "Works" throat,

"Damn, how you got a bitch working for you that you know nothing about?"

Kahladee

He shot back easy "She don't work for me, she work for Damarie."

J couldn't respond. She grabbed her things, told "Work" she would call him before she delivered if not sooner. J left "Work" with a huge feeling of deceit, but all he could do was go with it, he had too much at stake to even try to go against her.

By the time made it home her mom had cleaned, cooked, and changed all the linens. She left a note that simply read:

"Honey, please try not to let things get so disorganized,

next time, call me. Talk to you later. Love, mom."

J headed to her room while dialing the spa on her phone letting them to know to order Raneka a cab. She then texted Raneka, letting her know where the spare key, was so she could let herself in. J wrapped her hair, filled her whirlpool tub with hot water, added banana cream scented oil , and immersed herself in the water. It felt good to just sit and relax, she usually tried not to focus too hard on who the baby's father was, but the further she got along in the pregnancy, the more worried she became. She often considered aborting the baby despite Damarie's feelings but it was far too late for that now. All she could do was pray it was Damarie's cause if it wasn't, she knew it was over between them. J heard Raneka come in the house and immediately started yelling for her to come up the stairs. She had been sitting in the tub for an hour. Raneka came into the bathroom "What's up, chic?"

"Girl thank God you're here, I can't get my ass out of this tub" and she started laughing.

Raneka looked down at J, laughing at her and said "What the hell would you do if wasn't here fool?"

"Girl, I guess I would roll my ass out, but I know I won't get in here again." Raneka grabbed J a towel so she could dry her hands before trying to pull her up.

"You know J; you owe me for this one." The rest of the night J sat and listen to Raneka talk about her situation with Ja'Lee. She told J, she planned to lease a place first thing Monday morning, and she knew that having Ja'Lee locked up was the worst thing she could have done, and for that alone he wouldn't take her back.

Damarie rolled in the house at about 10am the next morning. He left his bags at the front door, eased up the stairs and into their bedroom. J was still asleep; he hit the shower, brushed his teeth, and slid in bed. J was sleeping on her side so he just nestled in with her, rubbing on her belly; she awoke reached for his hand kissing it. "Mourning Ma"

"Hey baby, how long you been here?"

"Oh just about an hour, I could have come in and took your cookies and you wouldn't have known till I was on top of you."

Kahladee

"Is that so?" She asked sarcastically.

"Yes ma'am, dat be bout right, now hand me the remote to the TV so I can see what's going on in the rest of the world outside of Raneka throwing my boy in jail."

"Don't even go there Damarie, he was zoning for real, hitting her, in public to make matters worse."

"Yeah well, I am going to get my boy out first thing in the morning so I can see where his heads is at. We not about to be all in their business either, we going to let them do them and we gonna handle us, so that means she can't stay here because it causes too much friction."

"Well for your information Damarie, she is getting a place in the morning."

"Well good." He responded turning on the local news. He caught the tail end of a story running, 5 dead in an apparent drive by shooting, on the east side of town, and one dead found 6 blocks over. No leads at the time, although the crimes appear to be drug related. Damarie cut off the TV, "Damn, all this happened since Thursday." He decided he would get some sleep before he called Mega, to see how things were going on the streets.

Mega was sleeping hard, but he was awakened by his phone ringing. He reached around and grabbed it and it read "PYT" across the screen, he answered, "Hey bay, what's up?"

"I should be asking you what's up? I called and texted you all night long you and you never called or texted me back. What the hell is going on?"

"Nothing baby, I had a lot going on last night and I couldn't call you, my bad, it ain't anything personal. Where you at now?"

"I'm at home sitting pretty wishing you were here with me."

"Yeah well baby why don't you get up and come over here cook me breakfast, and sit pretty with me, can you handle that?"

"Yeah I can handle that, give me 30 minutes."

Mija was already dressed so she just locked up headed out. On the way to Mega's, she stopped at a drive through and grabbed breakfast. The only thing she planned on cooking was his ego. Mega got out the bed ran through the house picking up clothes, wiping down the counters, spraying Freebrez trying to eliminate some of the blueberry Kush smell. He then went back to his room to put his guns in the safe and shake off his sheets. Mija was right on time; she knocked at the door while he was still in his underwear. He got up and opened the door, Mija was smiling "Mickey D's bag in hand." He was so tall that she walked right underneath his arm as he stood holding the open for her. Once she was in, he shut the door and pulled her back toward him and kissed her.

"Hey baby I missed you too" she told him. She walked in the kitchen, heated up his food, put it on plate, poured

Kahladee

him a glass of juice, and brought it out to the living room for him. She handed him his plate, sat next to him, grabbed his Kush and blunt off the table rolled it up for him as she knew that would be next after he ate. They sexed for about an hour and both passed out right on living room floor . Mega woke up about four hours later. He showered, dressed, and checked his cell. He had 2 missed calls from Damarie. He walked to his bedroom to call him back. Damarie's phone rang about bout three times before he picked up, "What's up bro."

"Nothing much"

"Mega, this shit with Ja'Lee is crazy, I'm going to go get him tomorrow morning, and then I got to go to Jersey to pick up 'Ryde.' She had to put in work on her own.

I didn't want the nigga to sit in jail for too long and it would look crazy as hell for you to pick him up. So let's plan to get together tomorrow night at club Seduce, talk a lil' business, have some drinks, and get our boy on track."

"Sounds good to me bro, my girl manages the champagne room, I will have her get us the best room."

"Nigga, yo girl?"

"Yeah, my girl, ha-ha."

"I didn't even know you had a girl."

"Well I do and the crazy part is her and Ryde are best friends and roommates. I found that out the hard way when I slept at her crib. Ryde came in from shopping or some shit and we was both looking crazy."

"Damn bro!" Damarie started laughing "How the hell you meet this girl?"

"I met her the night J and Raneka crashed the Audi."

"Man that shits crazy. I'm happy for you bro, sounds like your serious about her."

"Yeah I think I finally found her and I wasn't even looking, feel me?"

"Yeah I feel you bro, that's how it be, the ones you least expect, and when you ain't looking, well alright love face we will get up tomorrow as planned."

"Alright bet bro."

It was Monday morning and it was time to get up and out. The whole house was up and dressed and it was only 9am. Raneka was sitting on the couch with J, circling apartment listings in the paper when Damarie came down the stairs. He spoke to her, but she of shied away from him. He told her he was sorry about the problems she and Ja'Lee were having, and it would get better with time, and that a little time apart could only make things better. J got up from the couch, kissed Damarie on the cheek and asked him what his plans for the day were.

"I'm gonna go get my boy out, spend some time with him, and check the street credentials out. Then I need to head to my mom's today to give her some money and converse with her cause it's been a minute."

"Oh ok, baby what time you heading to her house?"

"After I get Ja'Lee out of jail? Why, what you got going today, Ma?"

"I'm going with Raneka to look at a couple of places, get a mani and pedi, and go shopping for the nursery."

"Well have a good day, Ma." He kissed her, grabbed his leather, and headed downtown to get Ja'Lee.

Raneka and J headed out behind him. They drove J's car, which was part of her plan. Once they got in the car, J told Raneka she could only look at a couple places with her cause she wasn't feeling the best, but she didn't want to pester Damarie, so that's why she didn't tell him. Raneka told her she would make it quick, "the first thing that I like, I am going to grab it. I can't be having this homeless feeling, so let's get moving." The first place was a glorified dump, the second was shabby and had a smell that made J sick to her stomach so Raneka took her home after that. Raneka pulled in the driveway so she could get into her own car, but J told her keep her car and said "just give me your keys, in case I feel better, I can meet back up with you or at least go get my mani and pedi." J got out the car, waited until Raneka pulled off and immediately jumped in her car. She let it heat up a minute, called Damarie and asked if Ja'Lee got out smoothly.

"Yeah Ma, he did I'm just pulling out his crib now, I'm going to hook up with him later so he can get his self together. I'm heading toward the E-way now so I can get to Jersey and back. Do me a favor baby; don't go too crazy buying stuff for the nursery."

"Ok baby, I will try not to. I'm going to stay neutral in colors, which I hate, but I got no choice, since your bighead baby wouldn't position right so what we could know what we are having."

Damarie started laughing. "I like surprises we will know soon enough."

Unbeknownst to him, J was five or six cars behind him watching his every move. They were in Jersey no time and just as she suspected, he lied to her. He didn't even attempt to go by his mom's house. He headed right for the airport and he parked and waited at the baggage claim area. J stayed 4 gates behind, watching. Damarie sat posted until out came a light skinned women dressed to the 9, wearing a pair of gold rimmed Aviator sunglasses. He opened the car door for her and took her bags. He threw them in the back of the truck and the headed out of the airport. J had to admit, so far there was nothing suspicious, he was always a gentleman. Damarie hit the e-way heading towards home. Although, she hadn't seen anything out of the ordinary, when J saw Ryde she was instantly jealous. She began to feel an extreme case of insecurity. By seeing her, she knew Ryde had brains,

190

Kahladee

class, and beauty. In three and a half hours later, they were back home and heading toward downtown. Damarie pulled up to a newer set of loft apartments and J parked about two blocks away at a meter and just watched. He got out the car, grabbed her luggage, opened her door, and when she got out, they stood face to face talking for what seemed like an eternity. J grew angrier by the second but she just kept watching. Damarie looked like he was going to lean in and hug her, but instead he pushed her back up against the truck, and began to tongue kiss and hug her. J instantly began to cry, she'd seen what she needed to. She was infuriated; she put Raneka's Acura in reverse. She pushed the gas pedal so deep into the floor; she damn there hit a fire hydrant. J sped through downtown, trying to hurry home so she could pull herself together. Once she was at home, she took a quick shower, sat on the couch, and started brainstorming. "I can't believe this mutha fucka is with this bitch, I helped him build this shit, how the fuck he going to betray me, I've been here, I'm going to send this Nigga and his bitch…I swear to GOD, I'm sending his ass…he's done!

Chapter 21

The Plot Thickens

Raneka called J later that evening, letting her know she found a place after seeing 15 apartments. Raneka said she was tired and needed to be alone and was going to get a hotel for the night. She also told J she would come back and swap cars and get her things tomorrow. This was good because J didn't want to be bothered, especially after all that happen that day. She got off the phone with Raneka and laid down on the couch. Later on, Damarie came walking in the house with 12 blue and 12 pink roses for J. He kissed her on the cheek and asked how her day was. She was noticeably quiet, but she knew she couldn't give herself away.

"It was ok; I started feeling sick so I came home after seeing two apartments with Raneka."

"Well can I get you anything? Want something to eat, or drink?"

He started to rub her feet and legs and she kicked him out of a lil' annoyance.

"No I'm good, I don't want anything."

Then she got off the couch poured herself a glass of ginger ale and headed up the stairs she didn't even thank him for the flowers. She climbed right in the bed. He followed her behind her, hopping in bed right too. She turned to him and told him "Baby I'm ok, I just don't feel well. I thought you were going out tonight?"

"I am Ma, I just wanted to kick back with you for a minute, is that ok?"

"Yeah that's ok, if you want to watch me sleep. Why don't you get fresh and go out and kick it with the Fellas? Trust me, I'm not good company right now, I don't feel good and I have to get up early in the morning and go to the doctor."

"Ok Ma, lay down and get your rest. I'm going to change and roll out. Call me if you're not feeling better later."

"Alright Damarie, J rolled over on her side, and fell asleep.

Damarie changed clothes and waited for Ja'Lee to pick him up. Mega was already in the club parking lot when they got there, they walked in together shaking up with everyone they knew from the hood, it was packed for a Monday. They headed to the back to their VIP booth, and took a seat. On the table was a giant bottle of Moët champagne and a card that read "Have a beautiful evening, I love you in a mega way, Mega, Love, Mija. Ja'Lee passed the card over to Mega and he wasted no time popping the bottle, filling everyone's glasses to the rim. Mega stood up and proposed toast "here's to brotherhood, getting money, and more importantly, staying sucker free." They all sat down and started talking about all the things that were going on in their personal lives, which they rarely did, but since they all had so much going it was hard not to lay some of the chips on the table. Ja'Lee went first, "man, y'all just don't know Raneka, done went nuts on a nigga. I hate I let her push me to the point of hitting her. She changed like the weather, all of a sudden; I was being accused of cheating, and all this other crazy shit. I'm glad I saw this now, because I wanted to marry her. I can't get married to her now for sure; she got that police juice in her."

Damarie stepped in, "And you know once they get a sip of that police juice, they start to drink it by the six pack. J's ass is just as crazy, she been sneaking around for months, just spending money, lying, and now that she got

---

194

Kahladee

my seed.., she thinks she's the first lady of slanging. But I did cheat on her, cause she don't want to act right."

Ja'Lee asked "Nigga, who the hell you cheating on wifey with bro?"

Damarie answered, "With the new future wifey Ryde." Ja'Lee started laughing I knew you wanted her bro I saw the way you was watcher her, Well I couldn't help myself, she fine as hell, smart, educated, good-looking, independent, and more importantly she don't got that smart ass mouth like J. I'm going to have her do this last drop with me and get her out this shit cause it ain't for her she just on some rebellion shit right now. And the last thing I want to do is created another J. After J has the baby, I'm going to set her up real nice, and I'm going to break it to her because it's over, we have grown apart."

"Damn bro, we didn't know you were keeping in, all that!" Mega said.

"To tell y'all the truth, after J pulled that shit with the house, I was done then, but then I slipped and got her pregnant. Well enough about me Mega got a wifey." They all started laughing.

"Yeah I do, and the craziest part, Damarie which you know, she and Ryde are best friends. I'm still shaken at that." Mega chuckled.

Ja'Lee started shaking his head "Well damn y'all, do they got another friend, sister or something for ya boy?"

Mega jumped in cracking a joke at him "Nigga, we can't hook you up right now, what we going to say? Date my boy, he will whoop yo ass."

"Real funny Mega"

It was about 1 AM and they decided to leave the booth and go down to the main floor before the club closed. As soon as they made it down to the main floor, Ja'Lee spotted a group of females and went over and started trying to holler at one of them. He was cut off in mid-sentence by a nigga talking bout she was his woman. Ja'Lee halfway lit, turned around and pushed the dude damn there over the bar. Mega and Damarie ran over when they saw the squabble, but by then two other dudes were all over Ja'Lee. Damarie and Mega ran right over and jumped right in and started swinging on the dudes. The other guy that Ja'Lee had knocked to the bar got up and leaped toward Mega, broadsiding him in the face. Mega was shook up, but he still managed to turn around to see where the lick came from. Once he turned completely around, he couldn't belief his own eyes, It was Chilla. They went at each other, throwing blow after blow. Mega landed on top of Chilla nearly making him disappear, underneath him. It was like watching a lion descend on a baby cub. Since Damarie and Ja'Lee had laid the other two squares out like blankets. They jumped in, pulling Mega off of Chilla which wasn't easy, Mega had turned into a beast, he was damn there unstoppable. But somehow they managed to pull him off. Chilla jumped up talking big smack. "Bitch, I'm going to kill you; I'm coming for you, best believe I'm coming" he slurred with his mouth full of blood and both his eyes black. "You knocked off my homie's and moved in on my concrete, nigga get ready to die" he spat. "I know what this shit is bout Mega you mad cause I perfected your technique, I'm getting money, and got your baby mama sucking my dick." The girl Ja'Lee tried to holler at just so happened to be Mega's son's mother and Chilla's woman. At this point security was there, Mija was looking at him, and his baby mama was standing at Chilla's side like she was some kind of "ride or die" bitch, but the truth was, she wouldn't ride for a nigga if you bought her the car to do it in.

Mega didn't respond to Chilla's threats, instead he walked away with Mija running behind him. He turned to her and told her to go home and he would be over later. Damarie and Ja'Lee were not far behind him. Once in the parking lot, they all boasted about how they laid the niggas out. But Mega didn't have much to say, Damarie and Ja'Lee didn't press him, they knew it was way more personal for him. They shook up and rolled out. Mega circled the block a few times, and parked his navigator out of sight and waited patiently. About a half hour later he saw Chilla staggering out to a baby blue Cadillac Escalade. Mega knew he rode alone because he always told him never roll in your car with the women you love when you're in the game. Mega knew Chilla was in love with Karen, he always had a crush on her, and even when Mega and Karen where together Chilla would always make references to her beauty. Chilla just didn't understand she was simply a sack chaser. And now

Karen, the money, and his un-loyalty would cost him his life. Mega waited until Chilla was damn there in his truck and ran up on him. "Bitch ass Nigga, who da Bitch now?" Mega asked him.

Chilla spat back "you still the bitch."

Mega looked him dead in the eye and shot him in the throat with his Glock 9. "Now shut your pussy lickers, you Bitch." Mega looked back to make sure there were no witnesses. All was clear, except the white boy in the payment box. He walked right over to the boy, pointed the gun at his head asked for his wallet, took his ID, and made him give him the video tape of the parking lot. He told the scrawny white boy, who looked like he was only about 25 years old, "tomorrow you're not going to come to work, in fact you quit, tonight is your last night. When the police question you, you say, I was masked and robbed you at gun point, after I robbed and shot that punk over there. You got it?"

"Yeah, I got it." He answered, still shaking.

"Well that's good that you got it because if you don't. I know where you live."

Kahladee

Chapter 22

Sent

Eight weeks had passed since all the chaos and drama had taken place. As far as Mega was concerned, everyone in the hood knew he was responsible for taking Chilla out. They were just were too scared to rat him out because they knew Mega had no problems doing it to the next man. He had slowed down and laid low since then because he knew that many people hated Chilla, but he also had a few that loved him because he broke crumbs with them. With Chilla out the picture, they had the north, east and west sides of town flooded with their product. Most of Chilla's crew started to work with Damarie and the fellas. Even though Chilla was gone, they still had to eat. Mega put the twins "thing one and two" in charge of most of Chilla's territory; they were hard workers and didn't mind putting a nigga on their ass if needed.

Ja'Lee and Raneka still weren't on speaking terms. The court ordered to Ja'Lee to pay a fine of 3,000 dollars, and undergo domestic abuse classes. Raneka regretted that she ever listened to J, because she was now finding out from ladies at the salon, that Damarie had been spotted on more than one occasion all cuddled up with some fly ass looking bitch. Raneka wanted to tell J but decided to wait until after the baby was born. She didn't want to send her into early labor. Raneka planned the baby shower, since J had asked her to be the baby's Godmother. She didn't know how things were going to turn out with her and Ja'Lee; she hadn't seen or talked to him since the incident. Damarie of course, asked Ja'Lee to be the Godfather. She knew they were going to have to get along for the sake of their Godchild.

Dameta finally sat down with Mija and told her the truth about her new job, Damarie, the drug dealing, and lastly that she knew Mega through Damarie as well. Mija was disappointed in her, but since she reassured her that she was only going to do the final drop and she was out. Mija had no choice but to roll with it. However, since the secret was out Mega and Damarie seemed to be over at their place all the time and even Mija adapted to calling Dameta, Ryde.

Outside of eating everything in sight, J had made following Damarie and blackmailing "Work" her new gig. She had "Work" sending her money left and right, made him buy her a town home in Atlanta, and also made him

Kahladee

invest in a savings bond worth 200,000 dollars. She was stashing and for good reason.

The morning of the baby shower J rolled over realizing that Damarie did not even sleep in bed with her. She jumped out of bed screaming for him at the top of her lungs. She waddled down the stairs to see if he was on the couch but he wasn't there. She opened the door to see if the truck was in the driveway but it wasn't there. She slammed the door and headed toward the kitchen to the house phone and dialed his number, it went straight to the voicemail, and she dialed his other number, that to went straight to voicemail. I know he's with that bitch, she thought, she began to pace, and panic. I can't believe he doing this to me, how could he? She grabbed the phone and dialed Raneka telling her that Damarie hadn't come home. Raneka told her to calm down; he's probably just with Ja'Lee. I bet they got drunk and passed out. You just relax J; I will call down to the Jail and see if he's there. If he's not there, I will drive over to Ja'Lee's to see if he's there. You just get ready and I will pick you up at noon, we have an appointment at Mac to get our faces done, so you can be fresh to death at your shower. Raneka hung up the phone, and dialed Ja'Lee to her surprise he answered, "Yeah what's up?"

"Lee this is Raneka."

"I know who this is, what's up?"

"I was calling because Damarie didn't make it home last night and J is in a panic. Is he over there?"

"Yeah he's here knocked out, we drank a lil' too much last night. What time is the shower?"

It's at two o'clock she replied. Alright no worries we will be on time. Text me the address to the venue." Ja'Lee went through his phone looking for Ryde's number, he found it and hit the send button, the phone rang for what seemed like an eternity, but she finally picked up in a groggy voice "hello."

"Ryde this Ja'Lee is Damarie there?"

She reached over tapping him realizing it was the next morning. Ja'Lee heard her say "Oh shit, Damarie... Damarie, wake up, Ja'Lee's on the phone."

Damarie grabbed the phone "What up bro, what's wrong?" Ja'Lee responded "Nigga what you mean, what's wrong your woman at home going insane because yo ass didn't go home last night, that's what's wrong." Damarie half in and half out finally realized it was the next day and the day of the shower. "Oh shit bro, cover for me."

"I already did, she thinks you got drunk and stayed over here so you better hurry up and get over here." Damarie hung up the phone and rolled right back into Ryde's arms, falling back asleep for another four hours, waking up at 2pm. He jumped up, ran to the bathroom throwing water on his face, and brushing his teeth. He ran out the door and took the stairs down 15 flights. He damn there knocked the doorman in the revolving door, down

Kahladee

trying to get out of the building. He jumped in his truck, turned on his phone, his text messages begin to pop up, he had 15 texts and 25 missed calls. He ignored them all and called Ja'Lee, he picked up "Man where the fuck you at? Your mom called my phone, your aunts, everyone."

"I'm on my way bro; bring me down an outfit."

"Damarie that pussy can't be that good that it got you fucking up like this, come on man."

"I know bro, I fucked up." He hung up the phone and arrived at Ja'Lee's 15 minutes later. Ja'Lee was waiting outside when he got there. He jumped in and Damarie sped off trying to hurry downtown to the Hilton. They made it in 15 minutes. Damarie changed shirts in the car, sprayed on a little cologne and walked in like nothing happened. They walked in the huge ballroom, it was packed full of family and friends. Raneka had done a damn good job; she definitely knew J's style. Damarie spoke to everyone that he could and eventually made it over to J. She was heated and he could tell. He leaned in to kiss her, "I'm sorry baby; I was severely drunk and hung over." She told him that it was ok and they would talk later. As he pulled forward, she noticed a hickey on his neck. She almost lost it right then and there but managed to keep her composure and just cry. Everyone thought she was crying because of the shower and all the people, their baby brought together. After all the games, food, and festivities were done, J made her way to the ladies room and sent a text message to "Work," telling him to set up the drop and make Damarie and the Ryde leave tomorrow. Otherwise she would be over with her Babies"R"Us gift registry in hand. "Work" didn't ask questions he just started making arrangements. She returned to the party joining hands with Damarie to thank everyone and say goodbye. Finally everyone was gone and it was just Raneka, Damarie, and Ja'Lee there with her. The guys loaded all the gifts in the truck, filling the trunk and back seats. When they returned, Raneka and J were waiting in the lobby. Ja'Lee hugged Raneka, told her she threw a beautiful party; she thanked him and headed for her car.

Once they got home Damarie knew J would start in on him, but she didn't, so he brought it up by apologizing again, but J didn't even bite. "Baby, I told you not to worry about it. I'm done with it, it's over." Damarie couldn't say anything; he didn't know how to respond. For the first time, J didn't try to argue.

Damarie was stepping out the shower when his phone rang it was "Work,"

"Hello"

"Yeah"

"Damarie, I need you to make that last drop A.S.A.P., like tomorrow, they are bringing down the house, so we got to get in and out. My father-in-law is selling the company as early as Monday. There will be buyers and city officials all over the place by Sunday."

"Well how soon do I have to leave?" he asked.

Kahladee

"I need you to leave out tomorrow morning so you can make the 12pm flight."

"Alright sounds like a plan, we will be at your crib around 9 am to get the money."

Damarie sent Ryde a text next telling her he would be at her house at 6am, it was time to leave town. Damarie finished drying off and headed back to the bedroom to tell J that he had to leave town. Once again, she didn't put up a fight, all she said was you better rest up considering your hang over. He didn't think much of it, set his alarm and went to bed.

The next morning Damarie got up packed a small duffle, kissed J on the cheek, and headed out to pick up Ryde. When he got to Ryde's place, she was already outside waiting. She had her hair pulled back in a sleek pony tail, and was wearing a burgundy and eggnog colored Juicy Couture velour jump suit. After Ryde got in and threw her bag in the back, she attempted to go to sleep, but Damarie wouldn't let her. He started telling her his plans to leave J after she had the baby, buy a new house, and go back to school, and stop hustling. He went on to tell her that everyone was not cut out to make in the game and he no longer wanted her on the squad. He had made the same mistake with J and he didn't want to do the same with his new lady. So Ryde agreed to come back and look for a new law firm to work for.

He was right, I put too much into my education to be doing this and the bottom line was I didn't need to. We made it to "Work's" house in no time. He looked different than he normally did, when we asked him what was wrong he told us he had come down with flu, and he was tired from working with his father-in-law. "Work" didn't have a lot to say, he made small talk about the drop, and he gave us a hundred thousand in cash a piece, telling us that we were only paying for half of a shipment. I didn't know why we were both carrying cash, usually only one of us did. I didn't question it, because Damarie seemed to be rolling with it. We got to the airport and started the check in process; it was a little busier than normal I guess because we were getting on a noon flight. We got in line like we normally did; I was nowhere near as tense as I normally was. I had gotten used to it I guess, stick to the plan, act normal, relax, and everything would be fine. The line moved in at a steady pace and before you knew it I was at the security check point, Damarie was four or five people behind me. As I got ready to put my bag on the conveyer belt, all if sudden this force was behind me pushing me down to the ground.

"Get down now!"

I didn't hesitate I had no clue what was going on, I tried to turn around to spot Damarie in all the commotion, I could see him out the corner trying to get out of the line but as soon as he tried to slide out, they were all over him.

"Get down now! On your knees, now dammit!"

Kahladee

They had me laying face first on the ground, in cuffs; I could hear all the people whispering "Oh my God, what's going on?" I was pulled off the floor and taken to a detainment room. I saw them take Damarie in the opposite direction. Once I got in the room they started asking me all kinds of questions, "Who are you? What are you doing carrying that amount of cash? Do you know the other gentlemen?"

I told them I had seen him before in passing and that we worked for the same company. Then they laid out my passport and ID. Telling me both were fake and they knew I did not work for the FDA. At that point, I refused to answer any questions, I knew we were busted. They read me my rights, and took me to jail. Once I got there, they stripped searched and fingered printed me, and threw me in a cell for about five hours. Later on, I was brought down to the integration room, again they came with a million questions, yelling, throwing notebooks in my face telling me to right out my statement. I asked what I was being charged with, I was told impersonation of a government employee, attempt to extort money and/or money laundering, and I was looking at ten years if I didn't talk. A police officer knocked and entered the room passing the detective a manila folder. He opened it, let's see what else we got ourselves, he skimmed through it quickly. "Oh I see, I'm not dealing with an amateur, I got myself a lawyer on my hands." I told him I wasn't talking and he might as well give up. He saw how serious I was and called a guard to take me back to the cell. I laid in the bed of the cell trying to wrap my mind around all of this, I don't know what went wrong, we did nothing different, and I just don't get it I thought. Then it came to me, we had been set up, but by who? It had to be "Work." He was acting strange as hell, rushed the drop, and changed shit up. I wasn't allowed to make a phone call until the next morning. I called Mija, told her how things went down and gave her the name of a lawyer to call for me. She told me she would get right on it and be up here as soon as they would let her visit. I knew right away that neither jail nor prison was the place for me. I became sick, I was throwing up, and I couldn't eat or sleep. I hated it, dirty bitches were everywhere and I had to deal with it. I got so sick that I had to be taken to the hospital. I thought it was because I wasn't eating. Unfortunately that wasn't case, I was dealt another blow, I was four weeks pregnant. About two weeks later, I met with my lawyer, he told me they wouldn't give me bail because I was a flight risk, and they were going to try Damarie and I separate because he told them we had no connection. It would be six to nine months before I saw a court date and I wasn't allowed any contact with Damarie. My lawyer didn't see this being a problem since we claimed we didn't know each other.

Mija came up to see me the same week as I saw my lawyer. She cried when she seen me, I knew I had to stay strong, if I broke down, she would sense my fear. She started talking so fast I had to tell her to slow down. "Ryde she said loudly, I mean Dameta girl, rumors are spreading like wild flowers, I talked to Mega, and he told me that they are around town saying you set this whole thing up, that you're the law."

Kahladee

"What?" I responded with my eyes spread wide.

"Yeah girl, Mega said Ja'Lee told him that Damarie believes this shit because you are a lawyer. They are also saying his girl is putting the shit in his ear."

"I just shook my head in disbelief; Mega and Ja'Lee don't believe it, do they?"

"I know Mega doesn't, and Ja'Lee don't know what to think."

"I told Mija that I believe 'Work' set us up." I then started crying and told Mija that the thought of Damarie thinking I would do this to him had me baffled. I'm pregnant with his baby Mija. She just looked at me not knowing how to respond. I told her not to tell anyone about my pregnancy. The last thing I needed was somebody sending a bitch at me to kick out my seed. Our time was up five minutes later, she promised she would come up often and keep me posted. All I could do for now was, nurture my seed, work on my case and pray. I would find out how all this happened and get even, it was just going to take time, and all I had now was time.

www.ingramcontent.com/pod-product-compliance
Lightning Source LLC
Chambersburg PA
CBHW070121260626
47160CB00004B/1564